THE. HOPE.

Craig Francis Power

THE. HOPE.

Craig Francis Power

PEDLAR PRESS | ST JOHN'S NL

COVER ART Coco Guzman, *La Memoria/The Memory*,
acrylic marker and ink marker on paper, 2013

COPY PHOTOGRAPHY Christian Bujold

DESIGN Oberholtzer Design Inc., St John's NL

TYPEFACES Gotham, Scala

PRINTED IN CANADA Coach House Printing

LIBRARY AND ARCHIVES CANADA CATALOGUING IN PUBLICATION

Power, Craig Francis, 1974–, author

The. hope./Craig Francis Power.

ISBN 978-1-897141-78-6 (paperback)

i. Title.

PS8631.0839H66 2016   C813'.6   C2016-900801-0

First Edition

ACKNOWLEDGEMENTS

The publisher wishes to thank the Canada Council for the Arts and the NL Publishers Assistance Program for their generous support of our publishing program.

Canada Council   Conseil des arts
for the Arts   du Canada

Newfoundland
Labrador

for Milan

DAY. ONE.

St. John's to Heart's Content

What are the colours of the rivers in heaven?

Lee Wulff, I wish you'd tell me.

Here I am a man of moderate talent but extreme good looks, sitting alone in my room, thinking of your bush plane hurtling, jack-knifing, abrupt as a colon: crashing out there, in the wilderness of Labrador.

Weddings, funerals, accidents. Medical problems. My heart like a bomb. And my guts? Let's talk about that later.

Tell me of the fishing, Lee. Tell me in heaven is it always cast and you pull that sucker in? Or is it a pool with a mammoth lying there where the current breaks over an upturned tooth of rock and you stand in the pull and the treachery of the current with the fly kissing the surface of the water forever?

Catherine says I'm obsessed with death.

She says it's unnatural.

Or else, when she's drunk, utterly natural.

What do you think?

I try my best to live an honest and quiet life. Not like her. Every night Catherine makes her rounds from bar to bar with her high heels and her bag of rolling tobacco.

She gets a call in the middle of the night from Istanbul wanting an interview. Beijing wants a visit from her at the university. Some cultural centre puts her up for six weeks at a nice hotel where they have handmaidens waiting to cut hair and go down on you—the girls peeling off layers while Catherine reclines on the leather sofa with the lights of that city, twenty million strong, glowing brightly out the hotel window. Catherine stuffing her rollie with the end of a match, thinking how rebellious she must look.

Cause that's the way Catherine is. She'll do anyone, given the opportunity. Or almost anyone, particularly if she doesn't know you well, and there's no chance you'll fall for her and make an idiot of yourself.

"I can't stand any slobbering and cuddling," she tells me. "If I wanted that, I wouldn't be with Martin."

So when she's travelling, lecturing at one place or another, she'll let the girls from the Rub and Tug go down on her like something from a pornographer's storyboard. She's had them all: university professors, waitresses, a janitor with warts on his hands and a face like a dog's ass, homely small town rock stars, sensitive poet types, union delegates. She likes pretty girls and butt ugly men. Dudes with busted knuckles and neck tattoos, chicks in ballet shoes whose steps are as light as dew on a windowpane—but the best are the trannies, Joe, baby, she says. I've never met a lady-boy I didn't like.

I wonder about your hands on the controls of that bush plane going down—down, Lee, like the heads of Catherine's handmaidens in a hotel room in a place I've never been. I wonder if you would've been Catherine's type. I've read your books. I know almost everything there is to know about you. I know Portland Creek. I know the names of your children. I know your world records. I know the fishing camps you founded just after the war. I know that you, Lee—American, wealthy, famous—helped start what has become the cultural tourism industry of my homeland—Newfoundland—the wasteland. I know the west coast of the island where the updrafts come out of the gorge as quick as casting a fly out into the river. Just snap your wrist and the White Wulff, or the Grey, or the Royal (my favourite), perches down on the surface and B A M ! —like that—the wind can send a bush plane flat on its back with the floats sticking up.

I know everything because my first task at the Gallery when they hired me was to curate a display about your life. They gave me a choice—you or Al Pittman—and I didn't hesitate.

A glass case behind which we displayed photos of you—smiling, squinting on a riverbank.

Handwritten notes from your time at art school in Paris.

A pair of your waders and a tackle box.

A bamboo pole and a life jacket.

And I wonder about the nature of your hands just before the moment of impact. I see the fine bones, the veins, the nails black with the blood of some released salmon: soil, fish scales, soot. Fingers gripping the wheel, the engine dead, the terrain, the spruce and the sharp needles of the branches tossing in that endless wind, the rocks and the desolate, terrible landscape coming up up up right into your face.

Lee Wulff, I love you. And the proof of love is evidenced by the fact I have thought thusly of your hands and how can love truly exist between people without consideration of the other's hands and of how they make their lively and delicate and exquisite flight through the world?

Dear Lee, the history books have not yet been sufficiently written. It may be that you were some sort of monster. Some sort of philandering bush man. It may be you had some collective of woebegone squaws or otherwise wretched outport girls in your makeshift fishing huts, in your virgin territory bungalows. It may be, that like Catherine, your appetite for flesh ran as deep and as disturbing as the gorge at Portland Creek. And therefore, there may be anything, and this unknowable quantity, Catherine claims, is the gasoline, the lift and thrust, that keeps us searching, that keeps her writing, after all.

Tonight, after Catherine went home to Martin, staggering zigzag mad and ranting from this little place I call my home, I got that ache and itch in the pit of my ass crack and could think of nothing but your hands, Catherine's voice, the next day at work, your hands, the cold and utter death of Labrador, caribou, Atlantic salmon long as a man is tall, itch itch, work tomorrow, the plane as silent as a stone dropped from some great height, sleep.

My dear Catherine, full of Blue Star, ruin, Ecstasy and God knows what else, until the lights go out and she awakens next morning with Martin at the foot of the bed with a cup of black coffee and her spit-lickies and a smile that is knowing and forgiving and hurt and warm and loving all the same.

For that is Catherine's life and this is mine and that was yours. Now excuse me, darling Lee, while I go out for a fresh two litre and will hopefully not be too strung out on sugar from my Sprite in the morning to go to work despite my twenty-seven sick days and the dental and health and all the rest.

For nevertheless, this here's the dangerous stuff.

This here's the real gold and the blood.

—— • ——

Discuss matters important to the larger discourse around contemporary art and literature.

> Take pride in your work.
> Subscribe to periodicals pertaining to the contemporary art world.
> Read these periodicals.
> Have a more informed opinion about these matters.
>
> Quit your job.
> Quit your job.
> Quit your job.
> Continue to work.
> Whatever.

I am the Adjunct Curator of Contemporary Art at the Provincial Gallery. What is it about those words that makes me think of heart failure?—an engine dying out over some barren stretch of bog land and you just hold on in hopes of an open body of water.

I hold on, seeing myself gliding above the hills, thinking about the currents of air beneath my wings. I think of coffee break, lunch, coffee break, quitting time, until I arrive at such a wonderful moment that I'm released and free until the next go round tomorrow.

My morning routine—portfolio show and tell—and because it's my last day before vacation, I'm actually pumped for what's to come.

She's freshly graduated, twenty-two, blonde and blue eyed and built and sitting across from me in my office—talking non-stop—painting, photography, performance, ceramics, on the top of my desk—the clatter of beach rocks painted red, she says, "for the tides and the moon and menstruation and love"—a hippie no doubt and delusional, yes—but man—beautiful—and dry, I notice, despite the last four days and nights of rain—so torrential in fact that I'm still soaked an hour after arriving at the office.

She slaps down a painting of a lighthouse and leans over the desk so that my eyes are drawn straight down her blouse. And she's saying something about this lighthouse—a two day camping trip, and hiking, the spirituality of the landscape—a beacon in the night—and while I should be listening, for some reason I'm thinking of nights on Portland Creek, how vividly the night sky is reflected on the surface of the water, and I start to feel afraid that I'm the one who's lost—that I've forgotten the geometry of the stars and am set adrift in the universe.

She stops talking. Sits back in the chair, watching me.

"Hope you like what I've brought you today," she says, uncrossing her legs, and when I don't answer, she's up, packing her things into her portfolio case.

I stand.

Extend my hand.

"Yes. Thank you," I say.

My voice like it's coming from somewhere else—a robot, statue or ghost, I don't know. I've already spoken to Doc Sparling about this dissociation thing that seems to be happening.

Professional protocol—I just don't get it, and my fall-back is to hide any idiosyncrasy—which is probably idiosyncratic itself.

The girl tucks a stray hair behind her ear.

I think of Catherine and a similar gesture she does when she's about to sink to her knees.

"Programming meets next month and I'll be sure to mention you," I say.

She smiles.

We shake.

I walk her to the door of my office. There's another show-and-tell in the waiting room. A guy, also beautiful, also dry and fresh and hopeful—his hair is perfect, too perfect in fact—it rains harder on me than anyone else.

It's a trick of the wind, I think, but my thoughts are interrupted as the boy begins to unpack his portfolio.

—— • ——

Pack bags for trip with Catherine.

Shine the THUNDERBOLT.

Read over The Motherfucking Bible for agent meeting in CB.

Research agent.

Destroy The Motherfucking Bible before meeting.

The car on the road and the road winding through the ramshackle neighbourhoods. Brightly painted houses of yellow, lime green, sky blue and red lean this way and that. Worn shingles, broken eves, dirty windows. In the spring morning air, the shrieks of children on the broken sidewalks, and our car passes them by, a gang of grimy preteens throwing empty rum bottles against a black brick wall in the beaming sunlight in an empty lot and the sound of broken glass echoing echoing as Catherine puts her foot down on the gas, the arterial highway now before us, and everywhere around, yes dear Lee, the soft hills clad in spruce and navigation towers that at night blink red and red again like the pulse and throb of blood that is a warning and a sign to everyone sky-bound or otherwise down here on the rocky, bitter earth.

Now beyond the city limits, the farmlands reeking and the steam rising from cows dreaming in the fields. Bales of hay wrapped in white plastic, and on the gravel shoulder of the road a girl with a scrap of cardboard upon which are the words FRESH MEAT :)

Catherine beside me smirking and twisting the cap from the bottle of wine she has wedged between her thighs, shifting gears, the sun making golden, dancing oblong shapes through the windshield on the dash and upon her face and upon the green stem of the wine bottle's neck as it emerges obscenely from the space between her thighs. The round open mouth of the bottle like an eye looking up.

One thing about Catherine: she has a drinking problem. I mean, *of course* she has a drinking problem. She's just so goddamn dangerous. Half the time the kick she gets is from watching people watch *her*, you know, dear Lee? Like the whole thing is some ongoing performance piece. I think about those early days in high school she'd come into the creative writing class second period of the afternoon stinking of vodka she'd nicked, she claimed, from her mother's "liquor cabinet." She just loved to announce that kind of shit. But it wasn't until we'd become friends and I'd seen the inside of her house that I knew her mother wasn't the type to have a liquor cabinet because whatever it was about the way she said "liquor cabinet" made you think of someone living in some mouldering Victorian mansion set back from the road glimpsing out at you from between the hickory and magnolias and weeping willows and a pocket watch with a note saying something like: I've given you not a watch but a mausoleum et cetera.

In those days, the afternoons in creative writing, the smell of vodka was thicker than the honeysuckle from any gothic novel you'd care to pick off the shelf from the school library. On a hard wooden chair, legs webbed in fishnets, thighs more often than not lolling apart, drunk in front of the class, Catherine would reveal her exquisite juvenilia, holding rapt not just her classmates sweating and struggling through their "journals," but even Dick Evans himself, (whose slight lisp earned him the cruel nickname: *the witing teachah*)—stuttering and shrugging and nodding his head compulsively whenever Catherine read and you could see she knew even then, she had it. The Power.

Catherine's house was just one trailer in a sea of trailers in a white trash neighbourhood way out by the Avalon Mall where the hum of traffic on the nearby highway made the damp air buzz with a mysterious radio static. A white and mint green caterpillar with cinder block supports at the corners and aluminum shutters rusted brown where the screws went in. No liquor cabinet thereabouts, I know, because one day Catherine took me there to show me her notebooks.

Here we are walking to her house back in 1992. You would have been dead less than a year at that point, Lee, your trophies, films and books already covered in dust. You crashing your Piper Cub in New York state and yet I still picture you falling from the sky into the wilderness of Newfoundland and Labrador. Heart failure—that's how they say you died. But you had the misfortune of being airborne at the time.

As Catherine led me to her house, I was shivering in my corduroy sport coat, something I'd taken to, to seem more professor-ish or something. I watched Catherine's cheeks turn pink in the grey afternoon. Skipping school, she lit cigarette after cigarette, never inhaling, the very first affectation of what would become a life littered with them.

Behind us, Holy Heart sprawled in an Eden of pristine green grass and shrubbery, and as we walked away from it, the fast-food containers, beer bottles, broken appliances et cetera increased roadside in direct and opposite correlation to the average household's net annual income.

After Creative Writing, she'd said, "Why don't you come over to my place? My mom's not around?" Cracked her gum, blew a bubble, scratched her white thigh with the tip of a red pen.

I thought: Y E S !!!

But I kept looking at my feet. I couldn't look at her; not now, and not the few times she'd spoken to me previously.

I still don't know what provoked her to ask me over. Must be that I found it hard to make eye contact with her, something I've noticed some girls find intriguing about me, like I'm some shattered puppy dog they can take home and be sweet to.

In my mind, there was some sort of fantasia taking place. The inside of my skull like a rock show stadium. The dark sweet purple air was alive with potential, was alive with the sweetly slowly opening eyes of lilacs, or buds, or flowers. There was a high-end light show going on in there with smoke machines, a roaring sea of spectators.

Even the up-talk she used didn't bother me. She was Jem and the Holograms. By which I mean darling Lee because you probably wouldn't know that reference—she rocked it out all the way. Those earrings could cut a jugular. Her teeth, dear God, her mouth.

"I can show you my notebooks?" she said. Smiled. I had thought, even back then, each night, quivering, about what the inside of her mouth might feel like. I had pictured her sweet face hovering in the darkness above me.

We wound up sitting on the floor of her mom's trailer, sifting through leaves of notebook paper, the edges raggedy from being ripped out and I told her I thought she was the best poet I'd ever read.

"You like Rambo?" she said.

"I've only seen the movie," I said. "I didn't know it was a book."

"No, no," she said, "Rambo? Rambo. You know? *Vowels? The Drunken Boat?*"

Boom. I'd thought it was Rim-bawd.

With the sun breaking finally through the thick mist of the St. John's autumn, finding its way into the trailer to gleam upon the kitchen sink, I brought these sad hound dog eyes up to meet hers.

"Yes, Catherine," I said, thinking to myself it was high time I got myself into the kind of trouble a girl the likes of which I'd only read about before can get you into.

And that's how all this started.

—— • ——

"It's meaningless. I'm meaningless," I say.

"It's not like you're not getting paid," Catherine scolds. "I know plenty of people who'd kill to be in your position."

"I'd rather dig ditches." I'm looking out the passenger window at the world whizzing by.

"Or what? Work on a farm? If you wanna talk about things being really meaningless, you should come to more book readings."

That farm comment really stung. That was in Spain, see, after all the bad things happened and Doc Sparling was like: You should leave town for a while, maybe.

"I'm completely handcuffed up there, Catherine."

("Catherine," "handcuffed," and "up there": Yes, Doc, yes, Lee: my sexual obsession.)

"I know, I know. Adjunct, right?"

"You know what the CEO says? Peggy, with the MBA from Western? 'The Provincial Gallery is not an intellectual institution.' Can you believe it? Isn't art an intellectual pursuit? Jesus Christ."

"She just means it's there for public education, that's all."

"Public education? If I wanted to teach a bunch of yokels I wouldn't have gotten the MFA in curating."

But this is the real problem, talking to her about these things:

Catherine's gone from Iggy to Trad. BAM! It happened overnight. Just as soon as the locals started to like her, and probably, for the first time in her life, she didn't feel like such an outsider.

Then it was Catherine Prince downloading Emile Benoit, Figgy Duff, Ron Hynes and all the rest. I was like, What?

Back in school we'd listen to punk before going to demonstrations together.

Protest songs for the social justice nerds.

Making anti-imperialist signs, first in Heart's cafeteria, later in the university's student lounge—Spank The Banks! Just Say No To NAFTA! Freeze The Fees!

And before I knew it, I Wanna Be Your Dog became The Star Of Logy Bay.

Then road trips with Martin. Days and days at cultural events. Was she buying this? Fiddles and all that? Don't know. Maybe, maybe not, but for a while there the N L touristic clap-trap literature said only CATHERINE PRINCE CATHERINE PRINCE CATHERINE PRINCE. Here, there and everywhere. Readings, signings, talks and who knows, ribbon cuttings—the opening of a new strip mall: there she is, my girl, a breeze through her hair, holding a giant pair of novelty scissors, the sun catching a silver edge.

And here was me, her and Martin a few years ago when Catherine's star exploded in supernova—her agent had signed her up for the unveiling of a new war monument downtown—how is that literary?—a bronze plaque on the plinth that says: PEACEKEEPING and a statue under a white sheet about to be revealed.

Me and Martin in the crowd with about twenty others—old-timers and their families, veteran types with enough medals on their breasts to blind you.

Catherine up there beside the statue and a government official, the Assistant Minister of Culture, a Canadian flag pin in his lapel, saying: Whether in Haiti, the Middle East, Somalia or Libya, in suburban Quebec at the future site of a golf resort—we've been there to keep the peace.

Applause, and with a nod from the official, Catherine yanks the sheet from the statue.

More applause, and in the sun, a towering soldier of bronze, his face a grotesque skull, leers at us from beneath his helmet—two doves about to take flight from his monstrous hands.

"I'm just so pleased to be part of this ceremony honouring our long and storied history as an honest broker in international affairs," Catherine said. "Around the world, Canada is famous for our dedication to peacekeeping, freedom and human rights. As someone with personal ties to our military, nothing could make me more proud than being here today."

As she's cutting through the crowd toward us, someone stops Catherine for her autograph.

I see her smile, that grinning skull behind her.

Later, when I got her alone at my place, I mentioned it.

"So how do you have personal ties to the military?"

She grinned.

"Remember Derek? Second year at Memorial? He was in the reserves. In Signals. Communications. Those guys have the highest aptitude in the Forces."

I vaguely recalled him—just another conquest of hers from years previous.

An old-school brush cut and an obsession with cryptography.

"Did you mean what you said at the ceremony? That 'honest broker' thing?"

"Pfft. Come on, Joe, don't you know me at all? But at the same time, I can't go around alienating people, can I?"

"By 'people' you just mean your market."

"Look—don't give me a hard time about this, okay? It's all fine and dandy for you—you've never had to worry about money your entire life."

I let it drop. It was dangerous territory. No matter my political leanings, I'd never really know what it was like for her.

I flip through the case of CDs.

"Where's the punk?" I ask.

It's a wasteland in there—fiddles and squeezeboxes.

Catherine says nothing. I'm glad Martin isn't with us on this trip. This is the point where he'd turn to me, sitting in my place in the back seat, and try to joke me into laughing. The three of us off to yet another event with Catherine's name at the top of the bill.

Now that she's hit the big time, hardly anyone calls Catherine Catherine anymore. Now she's referred to by her initials: C.P. The most promising voice of her generation. Her face not only in the local rags and on the television, but in the national papers, the Canadian literary blogs, an interview in *Quill & Quire*.

How do you convince someone that their trailer-park-white-trash-childhood-strip-mall upbringing is really, after all, where it's at? Catherine, the little girl, shit on her entire life, only now to be fawned over by every Cultural Tourism foot soldier the government can puke out. How do you resist?

This Road Trip. Her idea of course. Automobiles make my hands shake. They make the Down Below go Boom!

The Dandelion is known for two things: drunk English profs and sycophants. Catherine said herself there're hand jobs going on under virtually all the tables at each and every reading. It wouldn't surprise me if she somehow knew first hand. Every single book signing. Every fundraising bake sale over the course of the five days. Don't ask about the icing on those cupcakes! Don't ask about what happens in the hospitality suite. Pay no heed to the whisperings and rumours of broken marriages, STDs, orgies and Jell-O wrestling. Because Catherine already knows the truth and would further put her hand on a stack of bibles as witness and confessor for anyone who'd like to know.

"How can you stand these things?" I ask her.

"The CDs?"

"No. Yes. No. Everything. This local culture shit."

Catherine laughs. "I kinda like all that stuff, Joe. It's quaint. Sweet."

I don't think she's talking about the Jell-O wrestling.

But I guess Catherine's due for some extra back-patting, for a little ego fondling, even if it means suffering through five days of Our Culture and Our Heritage and the goddamn Trad music punching holes in your brain till the tissues collapse under their own weight and you're left with a skull filled like a bowl to the brim with porridge that used to be your ability to think.

But fuck me if I'm going to listen to this shit in the car when I'm going to have to listen to it live at the Dandelion—they bring in every wayward diddler and squeeze-boxer from whatever pissy outport backwater you'd care to find on a map of the island—hoping the music will set your mind into the proper frame, to lubricate your back passage in preparation for the proper reception of the bursting girth of the hand-me-down festivities to come.

I'm sorry, Lee. These rants come not just because *I'm* an ass, but *because* of my ass.

First time it happened, I felt faint. There I am perched on the toilet at work, a stack of photocopied artist statements on my lap—crunching a deuce as Catherine used to say. But, wait, what's this? Something not right in the Down Below? Am I giving birth? The water in the bowl has a tinge of pink, and I drop that stack of paper to the floor. Take the afternoon off. Which is spent with the television and an afternoon of scandalous talk shows ("Tyrone is *not* the father!") and the first of innumerable dosages of various salves and ointments.

Doc Sparling says, Stop pacing. Pacing only aggravates the problem. Doctor also says: You're trying too hard, stop pushing so much. Just let it happen. Stop the incessant commentary, the flippancy, the derision.

There's the usual suggestions, you know? Prep H, Epsom salt baths, breathing exercises or what have you. Not sitting for too long, not standing for too long. Not moving too much, not thinking, not remaining prone. No to silk underwear, no to cotton, no to no underwear. Wool trousers are an absolute catastrophe. I pop the anti-inflammatory pills rapid fire, and nothing seems to happen.

I go back to the doctor.

Where does it all come from, he wants to know?

It comes from my ass.

But I don't say that. I shrug.

Do you need a shrink?

Yes. Got that covered.

What is it you worry about?

I don't know.

Feelings of helplessness? Paralysis? Disturbing thoughts?

Yes, yes and yes.

Why?

Who knows, I lie.

What sort of disturbing thoughts?

I don't know. Disturbing ones.

Suicide?

Join the club.

Self-mutilation?

Infrequently.

Unhealthy fascination with death?

Define 'unhealthy.'

I worry mostly about someone finding out. You know? Like, 'What if someone *finds out?*' About what, you ask, dear Lee?

Anything.

But, in the agitated throes of a flare-up, it's someone finding out I'm a fraud. Someone finding out how awful and ugly I am.

To and fro, to and fro, to and fro.

My office cubicle is precisely twelve by twelve feet. Much more spacious than a jail cell. And blissfully, at least as far as my assistant is concerned, the air exchange system at the Provincial Gallery and Museum is second to none. I mean, it's perfect. There's hardly any air in here at all, in fact.

Here I am, sweating, pacing. Sweating, pacing. And the thrum from the fans above my head cuts in so quietly it's like the breathless sigh from one of my pretty, recent art school graduate girls. What is it I do in here all day, you ask? I wish I was someone else, but I also think about the importance of writing lists:

> They keep you focussed on the task at hand.
> You remember what's important.
> Your mind becomes less cluttered.
> Efficiency, productivity increase.
> There's a material representation of what's happening in your life.

That odour, what is that, Lee? Is that what turning forty smells like?

For a long time I misspelled *Fraud*. I spelled it *Freud*. Right up to the point where my MFA Curating papers about authenticity and Folk Art began to appear to have something to do with psychoanalysis.

Oh, oh, you meant *fraud*, my advisor would say. Is your spell-check broken or something?

Yes. No. Fraud. Freud.

That didn't really happen of course, but the Hemmies did.

The Hemmies, dear Lee. The Hemmies got me.

Here they are—heads emerging from the tender tissues of my backside, monsters from the tar pits. Diplodocus, brontosaurus, tyrannosaurus rex. Here they are, like me, caught in the muck and waste of a millennium.

And the bronto isn't even real. A fiction most people still believe.

Only you and Catherine know of my affliction. My curse.

But the real question I have sometimes is whether or not the Hemmies make me a more sympathetic character.

Discuss.

POEM ONE OF TEN FOR AND ABOUT CATHERINE PRINCE

When she touches me, I'm hot.
A CF Red and Yellow Salmon Fly.

Fire in the down below
Her cunt the mouth of some behemoth that takes me down
Quick as anything. She's the Queen of it all, my Catherine
And when her and I get down to the very bottom
Where the mud and shit of a spring thaw
Clog the arteries, and the tender fibres of our lungs
Stiffen up, then goddammit Lee,
It's straight-up smoke inhalation.

A car tire bonfire
The trailer park where she grew up
The pawnshop strip mall
The town dump,
All ablaze
Where I don't know
Maybe the smoke from the wheels from this here automobile
Martin's prized Crown Royal,
Are choking us both
To death in an embrace
Of grey-black gauze
Shot through with white
Where the seagulls dart and hook
In the beautiful blue air
Burning like hell to fill
Their red and yellow mouths.

—— • ——

Catherine clears her throat.

"All I ever wanted to read about was a woman with some kind of heart in her," she says. "The kind that'd have you hog-tied in a closet somewhere right now." She has her hand over her heart. "Is that such a terrible thing, Joe?"

"No," I say, "I guess not."

"I just mean that I'm looking for something and I can't seem to find it in any of the books I read, you know? I've given up on novels. I've given up on fiction altogether. I mean, do I need to hear about what some twenty-five-year-old has figured out about love again, cause that's how it feels sometimes. Like I've already read everything before."

"So, what?" I say. "So we're both totally dissatisfied with what we're doing."

She puts the car in fifth and we go on in the passing lane, and I imagine some random stone on the asphalt ahead of us, like some random patch of hard air in mid-flight, some miraculous piece of physics taking the car into the invisible hands of a terrible momentum and landing us grill first into a solid plane of slate beside the highway.

"I don't know if I'm dissatisfied, I mean, I've got people fawning over me from here to Timbuktu. But, anyway, you should pity me," she says. "For reasons you don't even comprehend."

"Pity you?" I picture The Bible—a stack of paper the precise width of my erect penis. I'd been keeping it in the cabinet at work, but now, it sits in the trunk of this car.

"Yeah, you heard me," she says. "Have any idea how boring writers are?"

"I've got some idea," I smirk.

"Ha. You're funny. No. You don't. You don't have a clue the pressure on me right now. And anyway, generally speaking, my crowd are about as much fun as a bag of nails."

We haven't been driving for more than an hour. There is a barren landscape that dominates this place. There are tough shrubs, sinkholes, watery deaths even right in the middle of the island. I watch it all blur by the passenger window. Soon, in the wild marshes, it will be rutting season. I think about how the migration of moose can be pinned to the rising temperature during spring and summer, and of how the poor beasts go further north just to avoid the fucking mosquitoes. You know? They go up there not out of some natural desire, but just to get away from those ravenous bloodsuckers.

Metal, plastic, shards of glass. At what velocity do the broken bits become dangerous? Fasten your safety belt. Crash test dummies hurtling through a windshield at only forty KPH. Sinew, bone, vital organs. Forensics says instantaneous death at the moment of impact, but how do you really know? Maybe by some miracle you lie in the middle of the highway with your guts strewn all over the asphalt, looking up at the foggy sky above you and you wait wait wait for the ambulance that never comes.

"What's the matter?" Catherine glances at me, drumming her hands on the wheel.

"If this is the case," sugar like you wouldn't believe coursing just then through the sad vaults of my heart, "why is it you wanna take me with you on this thing?"

"It'll be more fun with you there, Joe. And I thought you wanted to head to wherever your fishing hole is afterward anyway."

"Well, yeah," I say, how can I disagree? I'd talked so much about the west coast I was even driving myself a bit nutty. Salmon this, salmon that, sun on the river in the morning blah blah. Sitting at the desk at work I'd sometimes stare at that little idyll river on my screensaver and the hours would just roll on by. Sometimes a thought or two drifts through my head like one of those pretty little clouds right there in the picture above where the river goes out into the pond. Five o'clock comes and you almost smell the fresh air on my suit. At the gallery, this is called brainstorming.

It's mid-morning, a beautiful, golden haze over the roadside barrens. Rays of the sun coming down, great columns of light in the blue air, the tops of the spruce swaying softly in the wind and the highway like a black spear burning its way through greenery where here and there birds too quick through the passenger window wheel and dive through the branches of the scraggly, roadside trees.

Towns scattered along the ragged coast.

Conception Bay, Holyrood, Bay Roberts.

In the cold water there the rusted wreck of some foreign trawler. The black block lettering in Czech or Russian we aren't sure which. Great bright streaks of rust on the metal hull. Leaning gently to one side and towering over the little buildings of the town, they sell tickets at the bottom of the gang plank to tour the empty vessel, and here Catherine pulls over and a man takes our money and the town is silent except for the wind and the gulls whose ravenous mouths are open and biting the air.

Our footfalls on the metal gang plank, and the green waves visible beneath, through gaps. The man leading us down below decks into the dark, abandoned living quarters where the only light comes through the tiny slit windows and from the overhead sign for the emergency exits, casting everything in a blood-dark glow, shot through sometimes with the bright light from the sun.

She ran aground where the narrows of the bay jut out into the Atlantic and was towed into harbour and bound to the shore after the crew lit out of town to wherever they'd come from, leaving the residents with this broken down artefact: in desperation they decided to make it this sad kind of tourist attraction, because what else do these people have but accidents and bad luck, the man asks us.

Everything left untouched, he says, and sure enough here in the Down Below of the ship playing cards and bedsheets and ashtrays and discarded books and scraps of paper strewn all over the small rooms as though the men hadn't given a second thought to just leaving it all behind forever.

And I'm watching Catherine move through the dim liquid air, stepping over newspapers from several years ago and the empty cardboard sleeves of action movies that are scattered upon the floor, the V H S tapes stacked all around, and though it's no great tragedy what happened here, neither of us think to say a word and the man slowly and silently takes us back up into the light, into the command room where Catherine lays her hands upon the steering wheel and poses, squinting yonder ha ha through the windshield of the ship to where the tide breaks on the shore.

We drive on. The wind blasting in Catherine's window. The CD ends and she just pops another sucker right into the slot. She doesn't bother even looking at it, because, after all, is there any difference between them all? She doesn't bother looking at the road as she turns to grab another bottle of wine from the back seat.

Back before the hemorrhoids started I could sit for an eight-hour drive all the way through without the itch and burn and the biggest worry being a Mountie gunning us at 140 on some curvy stretch with a ditch to either side as deep as Daniel's Harbour Pond where, dear Lee, your son Allen took his first solo flight in the Cub when he was sixteen years old.

Martin's Crown Royal: it would be cliché to describe it as a coffin, but that's what it is. A big silver coffin a million times more lovely than any I'd seen before. Even more beautiful than the one I saw after the accident a few years ago.

In fact, right here, Lee, here's the place. Instinctively, Catherine speeds up as we pass it. It's really just a gentle bend in the highway, but don't be fooled. All you need is a wet road, a foggy night, maybe you're heartbroken and running away and a moose comes suddenly, horrifically out of the brush.

And then, just like that, dear Lee, you're packing your bags and just as soon as your obligations, both familial and otherwise (funeral, last will and testament, weeping, etc.) are dealt with, of course, thereafter, you're on your way to Barcelona where the heart of Spanish Anarchism was crushed almost a hundred years ago, and where, you hope, all your memories of home will be wiped out, just like all those tough-minded Republicans were way back in the heat and dust of a free Cataluña when Franco and his men murdered and raped and firebombed their way right across the entire peninsula.

— • —

I want to know the cleansing fire of a gas tank blowout. I want to know gravity. I want to know the pitch and tilt of the wings and a fuselage exploding over a forest in Labrador.

Over the hills and into Heart's Content. Catherine's foot right down to the floor. How is it that towns like this exist? Tourism, culture, recreation. Lee Wulff, see now the sad progeny of your work for the Newfoundland Tourist Board in the 1940s. *They grow 'em BIG in NEWFOUNDLAND.* On lunch breaks, down in the archives of the Provincial Gallery, I've looked at that slogan on the poster you advised them to release. It lies beneath a sheet of glass so that, by adjusting my focus, I can see my own face reflected.

A watercolour of an angler holding up a mammoth. My big mug beside it.

We zip right over the town's main road past a woman leading a donkey on the gravel shoulder. Otherwise, a ghost town. But for one week every summer, Lee, the results of all your work are manifest: locals bedecked in period garb, chopping wood, playing fiddles. Saturday night they bring in some rockin' dudes to play at a beer tent down by the calm seaside. Classic rock cover bands: The Boys Are Back In Town, You Ain't Seen Nothing Yet, Desperado.

I close my eyes and remember: Catherine listening to music in my living room.

She has her eyes closed, nodding her head. I feel like my heart has grown teeth—devouring itself. Beat, beat, bite, bite, to and fro—I can feel each bloody fibre tearing. Catherine of the fishnets, of the mid-afternoon vodkas, is actually, sincerely enjoying this?

Then I'm in the Provincial Gallery, this vault I work in, where you can almost hear that same kind of music echoing through the chambers.

And Catherine is into it. The fall of Barcelona, the genocide of the Beothuck—nothing compared to this singular tragedy.

Iggy Pop, if he were dead, would be spinning right now in his grave wherever they put their rock stars in the town of Ann Arbor, Michigan.

The Heart's Content Cable Station is a red brick house that squats by the road. We park the car out front and Catherine's eyes are on the building's sombre face. Two girls in frocks sit on a bench beside the door.

She's got all these points of interest, Catherine does, where she wants us to stop and spend some time. Something to do with knowing the place you're from. Really *knowing* it, is what she says she wants.

"This is our time, Joe," she says to me. "This is for you and me, you know? Time passes, people make decisions, things change, but this is for you and me."

We go up the cute little cobblestone path to the doors of the cable station. There's something odd about the look on Catherine's face. She's examining everything. I take it I'm supposed to be noting how observant she is or something. The artist at work.

And now, it's like we're moving through water, slo-mo up to the informational panel—Communication, Commerce, Culture.

Catherine puts her hand on the door knob. We go inside.

And it feels, just then, the hinges creaking, like maybe she's leading me into someplace else. Not some hokey way-stop-welcome-to-Newfoundland-and-Labrador-tourist-trap, but a place where everything, Lee, from you and The Bible and the Hemmies and the accident and the whole thing, EVERYTHING, is all going to get sorted out for me, somehow, to throw a little foreshadowing your way.

—— ● ——

She was leaning up against the brick wall outside the cafeteria, and me and Johnny Xerox were coming back from the strip mall where they had meatball subs for three fifty and porn mags without the plastic coverings. I heard her laugh. About what, I don't even know. She was standing alone there like just the most rebellious fucker the world had ever seen. She blew out this beautiful stream of smoke and squinted through it right at me and Johnny, who later told me I'd had a blotch of meat sauce on my chin.

Johnny Xerox, now there was a nice kid. His dad was chief building inspector for the city of St. John's. Johnny said his dad had a corner office overlooking the strip club and the pizza joint and he had a secretary with 36DS.

This was Grade 12 because Nirvana's *Nevermind* had just come out, and man, we had plaid tied around every limb and enough hair dye in our lockers to turn the harbour blue or red or whatever you wanted.

"There she is there she is," Johnny had said, but I didn't even really have to look, you know, Lee? I knew. Bam! Goddamn, her boots, Lee. The fishnets. The boots. Her t-shirt, upon which was written: I'M TOO SAD TO TELL YOU.

And that laugh. Ever hear of the Black Forest, Lee? Ever hear of The Fairy Tale, True Love? Ever hear of The Nightmare? Because that was her: virgin lost in the forest. That was Catherine. That was her laugh. That, my love, was the sound of a terror as bright as the smile of a woodsman's axe-blade.

But what really got me: that cigarette. I don't care what people say, it's hot. You know, Lee, back before the war, in the days of the Female Question, cigarettes were a sign of a woman's liberation, or so my dad told me—"One of the first and most successful ad campaigns in history."

But that moment, her eyes on us, was perfect. The whole world made for Catherine, but she didn't know it. Everything made for her, leaning there like that.

I sometimes wonder if it wasn't then, in the magnificent cold air of that October afternoon in the parking lot of Holy Heart of Mary Regional

High School, that I didn't become entranced with art because of her. That cigarette and those boots and tights, leading me to all those fucking low-lifes: the Artists.

And me there, looking at her, how tenderly I wept, from the ripe age of seventeen years old right up till now.

Catherine is sitting at the window of our motel room, checking her email, saying, Oh Joe, I feel so wretched, the empty wine bottle from the night before at her elbow. I feel bleak, darling, she says, a stack of tourist brochures beside the laptop: The Fourth Oldest Cable Station in Eastern Newfoundland! The Home Of Newfoundland's First Fisherman's Union! The Foggiest Town In North America! Things we'd picked up in only the short drive from St. John's.

"It's as bad as the publishing industry," Catherine had said, flicking the pamphlets one, two, three, onto the bedside table where the bottle had sat, unopened last night. "Totally fucking desperate." She twisted the cap and glug glug glug and even after all these years I couldn't help but watch her mouth as the bottle went up.

"Just think about all the people in the world," Catherine says. "Just think of them all, scrambling around like they do. Or Canada, just take Canada, Joe-Joe. How many do you think really want to be writers? Every retired high school teacher, every lawyer, busboy, waiter, janitor and doctor. But there's only a chosen few, aren't there, honey? And even amongst that chosen few there's enough shit to smother you right where you're sitting right now. Think of all the shit in this country. Honestly, I feel wretched, you know, darling?"

I slouch a little lower in my chair, flick on the television.

"Don't be sore, honey," she says. I think immediately of my ass. "I don't mean you. You're one of us, Joe." She puts her hand on my back. O Dear Lee, my sexual obsession, my object of desire, my Catherine. Laughter in the dark of the forest. Maybe, when you were alive, for you, it was the wilderness, the thing you love, the thing that destroys you.

Blah blah blah blah blah blah blah blah blah blah blah blah blah blah blah blah blah blah blah blah blah blah blah blah blah blah blah blah blah blah blah blah blah blah blah blah.

Sometimes I come inside her, sometimes not. Sometimes I don't even come at all, usually if I've had too much Sprite and the shakes, O Lee, the shakes—I suppose that's what it is—make the Down Below go numb.

How I hate the people of the world. Catherine says there's a little Hitler in all of us. The interior dictator behind a set of gears not right here in my head, like how you might picture it, but rather in the old pit of the Down Below. He lives in my pelvis, a kind of suicide bunker at the bottom of those thirty-three steps that make up my backbone. I feel him down there running the whole thing, and he's more like Franco than Hitler, a fiery Catholic military man from old Castille who makes the whole Down Below burn in the very same way that the Nationalists back in 1939 made the country scorch and bleed like my asshole does, like the way the fuselage of your plane may have gone up like a torch of freedom in the wretched, bleak night of a Labrador reckoning.

And poor Johnny Xerox, he took a blow to the head after high school and worked for years and years bagging groceries at the Sobey's until, I heard somewhere, they put him away for grabbing some girl's ass in the middle of the detergent aisle.

Also: this is why I love Catherine. She carries in her inside jacket pocket two things—the obituary of Rosemary Tonks, and a list that goes like this:

What Women Are:
- those who belong to the Emperor
- embalmed ones
- those who are trained
- suckling pigs
- mermaids
- fabulous ones
- stray dogs

- those included in the present classification
- those who tremble as if they were mad
- innumerable ones
- those drawn with a very fine camelhair brush
- others
- those who have just broken a flower vase
- those who from a long way off look like flies

—— • ——

Holy Heart of Mary Regional High School, circa 1992, I made my move. Last day of Creative Writing, as we headed out of class, I slipped a poem into Catherine's hand.

"This is for you," I said, except, nervous as fuck, something more like, "T-t-this is f-f-for y-y-you." Her hand was a tulip into which my poem went like a dancing bee. And because of all the stupid books I'd read, I thought I'd get her that way. The literary equivalent of a well-timed, well executed cast with a custom-made fly rod.

O Lee, her sweet face. Maybe I'm wrong and she hadn't yet discovered the Power, because her sweet surprised face blushed. She said: "Why, Joe-Joe, how nice," and tucked it away in a pocket, and linked her arm through mine as we went down the hall to the smoking section outside, and all of Heart was rich and red in the spring afternoon.

Problem was, I'd stolen the poem. It was from Jim Morrison's *The Lords and the New Creatures*. I felt tremendous guilt afterwards, for some reason, and proceeded to swoon and tremble every time I saw Catherine thereafter.

"What's wrong with you?" she'd said, later that summer, as we sat on the step of her Mom's trailer. Ten black garage bags, some stuffed, some torn, lay on the sidewalk. Rusted car parts, a skateboard broken into pieces, a thousand fast-food containers littering the ground.I looked at her hands.

"Did you like the poem I gave you?"

"Of course I did. Why do you keep asking? You've been acting so strange lately."

I kept quiet. She said: I love you Joe. I know you're still a virgin, and I want you to lose it to me. I want to bear your children. I want us to marry. I want us to be together, Joe, you know? Forever Joe, except she didn't really say that, she didn't say anything at all; in fact, what she did was crack open the bottle of vodka she was holding in her lap and pour some up while we watched the kids of her neighbourhood throw rocks at a discarded windowpane nearby.

I had to go home. My dad and I were supposed to watch a documentary about the Lowell Mill Girls, and I didn't want to be late. He'd gotten it from a friend at the University library, and didn't I want to learn about the beginning of the popular press during the American Industrial Revolution?

Well, no, I didn't, really, but nevertheless, I picked up my bike, and Catherine finally said:

> I'm troubled
> Immeasurably
> By your eyes.
>
> I'm struck
> By the feather
> Of your soft reply.
>
> Sound of glass
> Speaks quick
> Disdain.
>
> And conceals
> What your eyes
> Fight to explain.

She winked at me. Brought the glass up to her lips. Then I rode happily and full of hope through the filthy streets to my clean, quiet home.

—— • ——

During first year at Memorial University of Newfoundland, Catherine took a job at the liquor store. I'd go by to see her. One night I went to get her after she'd closed the place down. I remember it was in March because the clocks went ahead.

> She loves me.
> She loves me not.
> She loves me.
> She loves me not.
> She loves me not.

And I remember that we'd taken all the same classes so as not to be separated. She killed English Literature. She killed Short Fiction. She killed the Canadian Novel 1950-present. At Heart, we always sat together. I wish I could say it was because Catherine wanted to be near me, that she hungered for the warmth of my presence in her life, but it was only because at Heart the teachers didn't have the imagination to seat us any way other than alphabetically. It was one of the few times I applauded their lack of imagination (Penny-Prince! Our names forever entwined!). We maintained the habit of sitting together at MUN. God, how much did I sweat back then, dear Lee. Our in-class essays made me tremble, while Catherine just rocked them out one after another bam bam bam no probs.

Essays came back: much rustling of paper. I'd turn around and say "Well? How'd you do?" She'd just smile. Before long she'd had the Honour's Degree application filled out for review by the Powers That Be. Me? Ahem. Ha ha. I tried my best.

Describe disillusionment in *Araby*.

Discuss the notion of rebelliousness in Updike's "A&P."

Discuss "Blind Clem" in Hardy's *The Return of the Native*.

How does the idea of the unreliable narrator operate in *Lolita*?

Standard first year stuff that I struggled with while Catherine's beautiful hands moved across the page of those god-awful in-class essays, her hands, dear Lee, those sweet hands were the grace of her mind made manifest.

I went to get her at the liquor store. Dudes just hanging out there, sizing her up. *Who the hell has a fan club at the liquor store?* I wondered. Catherine did, apparently.

There was one guy there that night who seemed to be trying to read every label on every bottle in the entire shop. He just wanted to hang around near Catherine as long as he could, surreptitiously glancing up at her every chance he got.

She's mine, motherfucker. It was a humid night. Catherine and I stood with her co-workers while they finished their cigarettes after the place closed. She had a motorized scooter she rode around, popping wheelies and swerving onto the sidewalk whenever a traffic light went against her. That night she doubled me down to Bowring Park and we hopped the fence and went down to the river where the swans slept by the soft bank.

I had to make my confession. I had to tell her the truth. If it turned out that she didn't want me around anymore, then that was okay, Lee, I was fine with that. I was so foolish. I still thought I was special back then. Unique. So I couldn't go on living this lie, ha ha, that's what I'd been telling myself.

I remember even, God what an idiot I was, looking in the mirror in the bathroom of my very first apartment out by the mall; this run-down little place where I had two roommates with smelly feet. I was looking in the mirror and saying, "Joe, you can no longer live this lie," because that's what I thought I was supposed to be doing, you know, Lee? I was supposed to be all tortured and messed up. Wasn't that how Jim Morrison was? I had even taken to wearing a bead necklace like the one he had, but had passed on the leather pants, which may or may not have been practical enough in Los Angeles, but here, in St. John's, next to the mall where a highway ran by and in winter the piles of slush could swallow you in one big dirty gulp, leather pants seemed a little much. But, it was the poem, you see? That little scrap of paper I'd given her was driving me mad with guilt. O how could I have wronged her like that? How could I have been so dishonest, so impure? That's the thing that was bothering me, that I'd just copied that poem out of some book and didn't mention it was borrowed or what have you.

"I want to be famous," she said, "but not that cheesy Tom Cruise type of fame, you know?"

"Me too," I said.

"I want it to be, like, genuine, Joe. Authentic. That's what I'm after. I want people to know me and my work, and to just, like, have respect for me."

"I've gotta tell you something," I said. She was staring at the river, where the dim light from the moon was reflected on its surface. The mention of respect was just too much. I was evil. I was an evil poem thief. And she was my true love and O how could I be such a little Hitler or a Franco or whatever it was I was?

"I want to just, like, be an artist, right? I just wanna live and write my books or plays maybe, I don't know. Maybe I'll write for film."

"I didn't write you that poem," I said. It just blurted out of me.

"I should read you what I've been working on," she said. "I just started it, but I think it might be a book. It might be a novel, Joe, but I'm not sure yet."

"Remember that poem, Catherine? The one I gave you? I've been lying to you, Catherine. I didn't write it, someone else did." My lip trembled. I could feel it.

"What?" she said. I could see that I'd broken her heart. I could see how soft and sad her eyes were just then. Except not really. "Oh yeah," she said. "I know *that* Joe. Think I'm an idiot or something?"

She laughed.

In my face.

"Jesus," she said. "Whatever. Don't look so upset."

But I was upset, Lee. I was devastated. I start to weep. Yes, weep. I wept. O dear Lee, how I wept.

I think fondly and so full of anger now of that sweet night when something as silly as a poem could upset me.

God, I was so tender, dumb and helpless.

As I would soon find out.

Catherine put her arms around me.

I cupped her tit.

"Oh, I see," she said. "Look. This is the only time this is going to happen."

It was her turn to lie.

She took off the khaki pants that were part of her uniform for work. She wore no panties. She hated that term, maybe that's why she never wore them, still doesn't even now. I wept on. I felt I finally understood literature.

First, it was a blow job. Then we got around to the other things.

Later that fall, she met Martin.

—— • ——

Slutty, tough girls are my people. You are, you know. You are my people all the way.

I respect women who own their sexuality, you know?

Bitches ain't afraid, as it were.

It's true.

One afternoon in high school, I walked Catherine to her locker and there was a note taped to it: BIGGEST SLUT AT HEART.

Catherine laughed when she saw it. She left it there for days. "I love it," she told me. "I love that whoever wrote it doesn't even know how brilliant it is." I was there when she finally took the note down a week later. She punched holes in the edge and put it in a binder with a bunch of similar ones, which she later compiled into a text collage poem. She read it for Dick Evans in our creative writing class.

BIGGEST SLUT AT HEART

CATHERINE PRINCE SUCKS COCK IN HELL

CATHERINE PRINCE HAS AIDS

CATHERINE PRINCE IS A WHORE

WHORE

WHITE TRASH WHORE

CATHERINE P. IS A BI-SEXUAL

I FUCKED THE HOCKEY TEAM (TRUE!)

POOR WHITE TRASH WHORE COCKSUCKER

CUM GUZZLER

CUM GURGLER

NERD WHORE

MY NAME'S CATHERINE PRINCE AND I'M A WHORE-SLUT

FAKE BLONDE

COCKSUCKING DYKE

LOOSE WOMAN'S LOCKER

FEMINIST DYKE WHORE WHO SUCKS COCKS IN HELL WHORE

GO BACK TO YOUR TRAILER, WHORE

CATHERINE PRINCE: I LOVE YOU

THE ART OF THE PERFECT BLOW-JOB, BY CATHERINE PRINCE

DIE WHORE

DIE

YOUR BODY FOUND IN A DITCH

LOSER

FEMI-NAZI

TOO MUCH MAKEUP

YOUR MOM WORKS AT SOBEY'S

WHORE

CATHERINE SUCKS DICK (EVANS)

CATHERINE PRINCE: TAINT OF THE UNIVERSE

After Catherine read each page—standing in front of the class at the blackboard—she'd rip it from the binder—

Crumple it.

Drop it to the floor.

Much nervous laughter from our classmates, while Dick Evans sort of hid his lower half behind his desk.

In addition to the notes, there were rumours going around about Catherine and the entire hockey team. About the teachers, the janitors, the elderly priest who led the mass on Catholic holidays.

Ash Wednesday, Holy Thursday, Good Friday, Catherine Prince on her knees in the vestibule.

"The Body of Christ," the priest says.

Catherine slowly opening her mouth.

My kind of girl.

My dad always wanted to be ahead of his time. He came into the living room with a book in his hand when I was thirteen—listening to our record player. I thought maybe he was gonna ask me to turn it off so he could read, which made no sense—he could have read anywhere in the house. He sat down beside me and I felt a surge of happiness. He wanted to hang out with me. He held the book in his lap and looked at me for a time. "A sexual revolution," he started, "a non-monogamous revolution, will lead to an economic one."

The book he was holding was *The Ethical Slut*, and when he finished his speech about sex and revolution, he handed me the book and left.

A few years later, when it was my turn to show how ahead of my time I was, I loaned the book to Catherine.

Dear Lee, if I had only known.

Not so many years later, I was sitting with Catherine in her tiny first apartment, feeling like just another bonbon in the window of her candy store. Ready, whenever and wherever, to be devoured by her. Lips smacked. Fingers licked. Like a lump of chocolate left to melt and moulder in some hot beam of sun through a window.

"You, of all people, should be proud of us," she'd said, getting up from the bed. "We've been practicing non-monogamy since almost the very beginning. And frankly, honey, neither of us wanna go back." She went to the kitchen for the vodka.

"My sexuality is my own," she called to me, quoting from *The Ethical Slut*. "I own it. My desire, like my experience of beauty, is an important part of who I am."

"Non-monogamy disrupts hetero-normativity," I quoted back.

"Desire is the one true revolutionary force in the world."

Back at Heart, having once written to her about how stunning she was, and of how everyone thought so, Catherine said to me, "You think I give a shit about that? Most of the time, when it comes to boys, I wish they'd just leave me the fuck alone."

I remember every orgasm I've ever had. The head of my cock exploding in a white supernova over tits, faces, asses, bellies. From the first pretty girl I fucked after leaving Catherine for U of T. And then all the other pretty girls with whom I compared the depiction of landscape to the depiction of the female body before, after and sometimes during our sexual escapades.

The air-exchange cutting in while I masturbate in my office—all the pretty girls I've ever known below me in some idyllic English countryside—the leaves of the elms whispering in a perfumed wind and the soft, warm hills of green in a golden light. And from on high, floating by on some pink, cotton candy cloud, I let go with a veritable geyser of pearls upon their waiting heads.

Preparation H.
Honey.
Ibuprofen liquid gel caps to reduce swelling.
Doctor's appointment?
Avoid seeing doctor.

Go to gym.
Jog.
Take on a more positive disposition.
Eliminate Sprite from daily routine.
Smile more.

Catherine had hardly fucked anyone in high school. I mean, she hated her fellow students, but I have to say I sometimes wondered if she hadn't banged one or two of the teachers, the way they sometimes carried on (and because of what I learned later: GoD).

"I'd hit you, but you haven't washed in a week," was one thing said to Catherine, by one pretty boy back at Heart, who now teaches, oddly enough, at the University of Toronto in the Business Department.

I was there with her, in the smoking section conveniently supplied by the Powers That Be round the back of the school.

After I'd seen her there that first time, I'd taken to hanging around out back, pretending to smoke, coughing, waiting for her during lunch break to arrive, whereupon I'd try and fail and try to muster up enough courage to say something to her.

But eventually, I did.

Me: I weally wike your witing.

She hid her smile behind a fake yawn.

Her: Oh really?

Tap, tap, her long finger on her cigarette.

Ka Boom.

Me: Yeah, no, really, I do.

Ka Boom.

The guy's name was Timothy. His dad wrote the business editorials for *The Telegram*. I knew that because my dad showed me his picture one afternoon after supper—"The face of the enemy, Joseph," my dad had said, the tip of his nic stained index finger on Timothy's dad's lantern jaw.

"The Business press," he said, "is the best one to read because it is the only kind of mainstream journalism obliged to give its constituency an accurate picture of the world." Then, right beside my biography of John Keats, he left the paper there on the dining room table for me.

There was Timothy's dad's little photo every Sunday, next to a headline saying something like NOW'S THE TIME TO INVEST IN LOCKHEED MARTIN. Timothy and his old man were twins, so I knew who he was, and then, boom, what do you think happened next, Lee? After little Timothy says this to Catherine Prince?

It was love. That's what it was. True, Motherfucking, Love. Me standing there watching her. And what she did next.

She head-butted him.

Poor Timothy's nose exploded.

Blood like ribbon flying out.

Ticker tape.

A red bow, like a gift.

A big surprise.

A red mist patterned my forearm.

Crunch.

Stepping on a bug.

Ka Boom, True Love, that blood coming out.

I remember that instant her forehead connected—she was a smiling animal.

Poor Timothy seemed to crumple, you know? Sucker just collapsed, and everyone stared.

Catherine, a smudge of red on her face, dropped her cigarette and stomped it.

Then she turned without a word while Timothy's buddies helped him up, and went back into the school.

Now here's a picture of Timothy on the U of T staff directory web page, what once was the perfect straight line of his nose an overripe banana.

True, Motherfucking, Love.

—— • ——

Look, I know what you're thinking. You're thinking this is probably the best novel you've ever read. I know, I know. Genius, like car accidents, can just happen, like an act of God.

But like Catherine says, the beginning is the easiest shit. Even genius will only take you so far. And while these first pages are, I admit, spectacular, engaging, beautiful, funny, tragic et cetera, I've only just begun, as it were.

There's still a ways to go before we get to the end, till we get to Portland Creek, and I'm not really sure what's going to happen, you know? It's totally TBD, just like my superiors at the Gallery say when they don't have a clue what it is we'll be programming next year.

And while I may be too old now to be considered a wunderkind, maybe little Joe Penny will, for once, not fuck it up somehow, and it'll be my picture in *The New Yorker* with a headline above it saying: THEY GROW 'EM BIG IN NEWFOUNDLAND.

And furthermore, my lovelies, if you're thinking about it, fucking up, I mean, I would advise you to not. Or, I don't know, go ahead, if you wanna. It may work out for you eventually. All I'm saying is that right here and now, I'm going to try not to. I'll let you judge for yourself how successful I am. And, after all, fucking up, like car accidents, can lead to a little shard of genius, a tiny jewel of broken glass, just like the one you've got in your hands right now.

And I haven't even gotten to what happened with the accident yet.

—— • ——

After the Heart's Content cable station, Catherine's hungry, so we find our way to one of those salt of the earth mom and pop fish and chips places where at night there's a cover band pumping out the Eagles with a U2 or two thrown in just to show they're hip, ha ha, I guess, but during the day, there are plastic gingham tablecloths and a wall of bamboo blinds that demarcate the dining area from the dance floor.

At night here things get tight, no doubt. Boys with the salt and the fish scales tattooing their forearms, smoking joints out back and coming in to find the girls in their Sears catalogue special order skirts, grinding it out under a twenty dollar light show. That wind coming in right off the water through the back door propped open with a case of Labatt Blue, and there's an eon or two of I've-got-a-bone-to-pick-with-you soap opera tension in the air, since, man, there's like only two hundred people living in this town and with a gene pool this small, trouble spreads as fast as fire or an STI, and the options for love or a quick fuck so tiny that yes, dear Lee, dear mainland readers, everyone really is related somehow.

But right now, daytime, we're both hip deep into our two piece fee and chee as they say, Catherine going all out with dressing and gravy that pools in the corners of the cardboard take-away container. Then in he comes, I guess Heart Content's' closest approximation to a pretty boy: denim jacket, James Dean hair, Chuck Taylors and a Talking Heads t-shirt, and Catherine goes a bit agog over the whole thing.

An anomaly, this boy, in a town where, I don't know, from what I've seen, baseball caps with snowmobile brand names and wraparound, mirrored sunglasses seem to be the thing, and he leans on the bar where you order your take-away like some Newf Tom Verlaine, you know? Just like some CBGB waster hanging out in a bathroom stall, and I'm mid-sentence, talking about Peggy MBA up at the Gallery, and I can already tell she's not listening, of course she's not listening, she was hardly listening before Tom Verlaine came in. Because this boy also happens to be just about as pale as the belly of one of these here cod we're eating, fresh like, wherever they dragged it up from, and that's just Catherine's thing, this guy, as pretty as one of the girls she usually goes for, he is, but she lets him order and wait and go out the door again without so much as a glance at us, because, I know, from a long and sad experience with her, that this Tom Verlaine type isn't what she's usually down with or whatever. I mean, like I've said, she's all about one of those skidoo types we'd already seen, ugly fuckers driving their dad's pickups around where the water comes up to the shore with a cup of Tim's at the ready and the—I don't know, Lee—Blink 182 or whatever blasting out the windows.

"Let's go for a swim," she says just then, scooping up the last bit of dressing from that paper bowl.

And we're out the door, into the sunshine, and at the edge of this secluded river when Catherine strips down naked as I watch from a rock in the shade of an overhanging tree because swimming has never been my thing.

Something about drowning, of course, that's what bothers me. Feeling literally out of my depth, which, in a way, dear Lee, is what being around Catherine is always like for me. And sitting here, my ass throbbing on the shore, I remember back when I was a kid, how my dad saved me from drowning when I was little, out at Cochrane Pond, and maybe that's where all my hesitation and paralysis comes from, you know?

But I'm not gonna die, all right? Just so you know. I'm gonna keep living, no matter what happens.

And then later, how perfectly terrible life can be, after she comes out of the river brown and glistening, when we're driving back to our motel, there's our little Tom Verlaine by the side of the road, thumbing into the next town over, and how can Catherine not stop and pick him up, and how, furthermore dear Lee, can she not take him, after some small talk laden with innuendo ("Yeah, I know who you are," he says. "I read your book last semester"), by his soft hand down the alleyway behind a dollar store to do whatever it is she wants with him, while I sit, suffocating, lungs full of blue, weeping, dear Lee, in the passenger seat waiting and waiting with the classic rock radio station cranked to the top and my head on the dash while the red and bloody sun pitches downward toward the horizon. "It's a paper love," she says, later still, me and her sharing the lone king-sized bed clutched as we are between the walls of wood panelling in the rundown little place we've rented. "It's a fucking imaginary magnetism. It's bullshit, but it works. It's made up like I am. Like everything."

She gets up and tears through our luggage. I hear my pill bottle roll across the floor. She lights a sparkler, one of the ones we'd gotten to celebrate the road trip, and the bright blossom is on up the walls and ceiling in a strange fireworks display.

"You know what I mean, Joe-Joe?" She waves that thing like a wand, and abracadabra: the letters L O V E dance from the bright end of the sparkler so that right there, hovering in the dark air of the room is that word fading from yellow to orange to red and then purple.

And right now, this morning, I can still see the afterimage flitting around inside there, every time I close my eyes.

——— • ———

"I'm gonna ask Martin to marry me." The spoon she's holding drops onto the tabletop, like, boom, the end, suckers.

"What?" My ass, cased in nothing but wool trousers, throbs like a heartbeat. We're at a café on the main street of the town, called The Wave. The place is rustic, yet elegant. Honest, or at least is striving to be these things. Lots of exposed wood. Mismatched antique shop cutlery, fireplaces, curtains your nan would have liked.

"Yeah, fuck it. I sometimes wonder why I've waited as long as I have."
Her eyes flash at me.

"But what?" I say again. It's a bright, glorious day.

"Well, Christ, Joe-Joe. I mean, come on."

I fold my napkin and put it neatly beside my plate.

"You don't understand, and that's fine. At least Martin tries to accept
me for who I am and not what he thinks I should be or something. I tell
him everything and he does likewise. Take yesterday. He'll know as soon
as I see him. He loves the gory details. He loves it all. We're beyond all
that ownership shit. We're as free as we wanna be."

She gestures to the waitress. Points into her mug. I nod my head.

"That alleyway was private property," I say. My cup goes down too hard
onto the table. "Someone comes out their back door, you're dead."

"Property is theft," she says, mocking me. "As a recipient of my
generosity, you needn't worry. I still have a lot of love for the world."

She's got this little gleam and this little smile.

"I still believe in beauty. Do you? Or do you believe in war?"

"What does that even mean," I say.

"How much have you changed," she says. "Are you still my little Joe-Joe,
or are you someone else now?"

I don't understand what's happening here. There's some weird bitterness
in her voice. I'm being accused of something and I don't know what it is.

A tense silence hangs in the air. I picture the dark forms of salmon
trying to jump some impossibly high waterfall. Catherine's tongue comes
out and whips around her lips excitedly. She brings the tip of her tongue
up to the point of a canine. A sad pile of bones on her plate.

"I feel like I'm getting on your nerves," I say.

This is code for: You are getting on my nerves.

So many code words, Lee, just like you must have had.

The waitress refills our mugs and Catherine's brown eyes linger
momentarily on her face. She's a hot little thing with a mole over her lip
and a sway to her walk that reminds me of one of my gallery girls.

"Holy fuck. This is God's country. This is travel, eh Joe? I told that kid last night about Georges Bataille." She pauses and looks at me. "He'd never heard of Georges Bataille. What do they teach kids these days?" She smiles up at me from under her eyelashes.

"Not everyone's like you," I say. "The way you were."

I can't stop looking at her mouth, that pile of bones. "I don't get it," I say.

"What? Marriage? You know me, Joe, I've always been a romantic. I like the ceremony, if nothing else. Martin's a good man. He can cook. He wants a baby and who am I to refuse a man what he desires?"

I can never usually tell whether she's joking or not, but this time she's serious.

"I mean, just imagine how strong he must be, Joe. You're my best and oldest friend. But you're more than that, aren't you? And he's never even gotten jealous. Like, not even once."

So whatever—I'm just gonna stare at the pattern on the floor.

"Don't make that face," Catherine says. "It's not about believing in something. Like some cult member." The bone from her final chicken wing goes plop onto the pile. "It's more about wishing something like that were real, you know, honey? What could be more free than freely submitting to something larger than yourself?"

I raise my hand for the bill, and feel inside me a thousand lights wink out. Because I get suddenly what this road trip is really about. It's like, Goodbye, Joe. It's, Catch you later. It's Jim Morrison's shitty croon saying This. Is. The. End.

—— • ——

Right now we're on the highway again and I can feel Catherine working herself up. On the CBC there's a woman reading from her new book—Kathryn Borel, I think—whose work is just the best—while my Catherine's about to bite right through her bottom lip, her rising blood pressure turning the car into a pocket of molten ash.

"Do you know what Canadian literature means?" she says, flicking off the radio. "I mean, Jesus Christ, Joe-Joe, it's like a brand of kitchen knives."

I can't help but chuckle.

She glares at me.

"You're just saying that because she's your competition," I say. "And she's got your name."

"Canadian—female circumcision," Catherine spits. "Repressed busybodies. I mean, even that word, 'Canadian.' It sounds like getting castrated. Getting the cunt ripped out of you."

I'd never really thought about it before.

"Is what the world needs right now another story about someone standing wistfully at the edge of some body of water, like having an epiphany or whatever? Like, seriously?"

I think: Don't go to the dark place, but she always does.

Carlo Rossi Red. The wine she picked up this morning. A three-litre bottle for, like, fifty cents or something. I watched her hands pour it up into her thermos earlier before we got back on the road again, and now this rant, despite how very good all those busybodies have been to her.

But this anger of Catherine's is a relatively new development—she'd never really cared where a writer was from before—as long as they made her throb.

Her teeth red and purple. And there out the window in the marshy barrens along the highway, red and purple moss clinging to the rocks that jut up out of the wet ground.

We swerve, I think of my Jess, the line of the highway a yellow ribbon.

> Have more patience.
> Have more empathy.
> People are fallible.
> You are a person.
> You are fallible.

Forget her.

Attain a normal friendship.

Support her without resentment.

Say something nice to/about Martin.

Destroy their relationship.

POEM TWO OF TEN FOR AND ABOUT CATHERINE PRINCE

UNTITLED

X-ACTO.
Gyproc.
Stud finder.
I slip the little black device into her hand.
"It'll find the beams for you."
Catherine helping me reno this dump
And before long
She drops the thing onto the floor and says
"I'd rather listen to the wall, and tap."
So what—
I'm happy just having another set of hands
And take off upstairs
Where there's a whole fucking room I have to take apart,
And the most bizarre ad hoc electrical I've ever seen,
Wires just totally wild,
And horsehair plaster,
Newsprint in the walls,
And what else—
Who knows?

But once I'm pulling that sucker apart up there
You know,
Just another line or stud or beam or stanza for the fire
Or the junk pile,
I forget all about her until later,
When I come back down to the living room
And she's still there

With her ear pressed to the wall
And I wonder
How long has she been standing there like that,
Listening for something?

— • —

I arrive at the party alone.

It's night, so cold I can already feel frost in the air.

Thriller playing out the speakers so the windowpanes rattle. I hear them as I come up the steps to the house.

Jack-o'-lanterns and black and orange streamers in the front door and inside all I see are the silhouettes and darkened shapes of dancers, drinkers, a few kids I recognize from class.

Dead bodies, ghosts, black cats and bad luck—I'm in hip waders and a checked shirt—Lee Wulff, like he'd stepped out of a photograph from a 1960s adventure magazine.

I hate parties and the people who go to them. But I love complaining about how shitty and boring parties are—which is why I'm always attending.

It's so loud my feet throb from the bass drum pulse in the floorboards, and I'm looking for Catherine, who I know has to be around somewhere.

And I'm not here five minutes when suddenly at my elbow, here's GoD. Gordon Devereux, the creative writing prof at Memorial—dressed as the devil—saying to me: "Are you Joseph Penny? I know your father."

What is he even doing here?

GoD—based on the vintage photos of students and staff at Memorial that line the hallways of the English department, was once a handsome man prone to ascots and sideburns and—if what the rumours said were true—liked his women undergraduate.

"Yes, I'm Joe Penny," I say.

"I'm proud to be a fascist!" he shouts, and I'm wondering if he's just in character or something, but the music's too loud to hear what he's saying.

So he leads me out the back door onto the deck where it's quieter, and begins nattering on—he's like, totally bombed—about how he and dad met at some gathering of NDP volunteers or some shit, even though, as GoD says to me just then: "We both agreed that while the Dippers have some seriously reactionary elements, they're a good first step in the right direction. Or the left har har."

Meaning anarcho-syndicalism. The ultimate goal. You know, worker ownership of factories, reinstatement of the laws against capital flight (See: Glass-Steagall), collaboration amongst disparate communities et cetera. The eventual dissolution of the state. Fair, as opposed to Free, Trade. The actual rule of international law. The end of Palestinian occupation. Something even vaguely resembling justice in the world.

And I remembered, standing with GoD under the stars, how when I was a teenager dad gave me for a birthday present one of those Republican propaganda posters from the Spanish Civil War. I still have that sucker, right above my desk at work, where I sweat and curse and think of you, dear Lee. Durruti looking out at the horizon with a clutch of young, hot-looking anarchists in the background waving black and red flags. The CNT and the FAI. Pretty Spanish girls with skirts up to here and rifles on their shoulders. Lips, ha ha, like red wine or something.

And then Catherine comes in wearing a wedding gown.

It's already a little dirty from the revelry—the lace hem and the train torn and dead leaves caught in the fabric. White evening gloves up past the elbow, and the thing that really gets me—a white ribbon choker around her neck.

I see her before she sees me, and as GoD talks on, I try to catch her eye, but it's no use. She's too busy talking to her date—Martin, the groom, in a full-on tuxedo that's about two sizes too big for him. He can't be more than twenty-two, and yet, across the crowded back deck I see the little paunch jutting over his belt.

Catherine finally notices me, and we meet halfway across.

"Lee Wulff," she says. "What a hunk you are."

We hug.

"Who's the troll?" I say over her shoulder, watching him—he's kinda fiddling in his pocket for something.

"His name's Martin. Engineering. He seemed kinda dull at first, but he's got great coke. You want some? I can get him if you like."

"Gordon Devereux's here. He's plastered."

"Oh God," she says, "Really?"

I glance over my shoulder. GoD slouched against the railing with his glass of Pimm's and his pitchfork, staring at us. Catherine's got this strange look on her face—something between exasperation and amusement.

"What is it?" I ask her.

"It's nothing," she says, and then: "I let him finger-bang me once, last semester."

She laughs kind of bitterly.

"What? Are you kidding?"

"Yeah, no. That's why he's here, I guess. He's maybe hoping it's gonna happen again."

She tries to smile, but it's more a grimace.

"Don't get all manly on me here." She puts her hand on the spot where my jaw is clenching. "I'm just telling you the truth."

What a beautiful night. A thrill of happiness goes through my bones—she talked to me like I was her boyfriend.

But later, here we are, the three of us: me, Catherine and the troll, squat into the backseat of a taxi after the party. Catherine's gown bunched up where she's sitting on the bump with her knees yawning apart and Martin's lazy eye jiggling around with every pothole.

Here we are, me thinking of GoD with his finger right up to the last knuckle in the burning honey pot of my true love who's so blotto right now, her head goes from my shoulder to Martin's like the bulb of a tulip in a windstorm.

And as we drive, out of the corner of my eye, I see them start to kiss—intermittent light from the passing streetlights on Catherine's face—tinny techno playing on the cab's radio—Catherine's heavy-lidded eyes closing, her sooty eyelashes—her hand coming up to Martin's cheek—and I say to the cabbie, Stop the car, please. Sir, please stop the car—but he can't hear me at first, I guess, because it goes on for quite a while.

They let me out under the blue florescent of Sears in the parking lot of the Avalon Mall. I watch the taillights of that cab surrender into the mess of neon and streetlights down Kenmount Road before hiding out behind the supermarket dumpster, and up she comes, a whole night's worth of cheese plate and too much beer (this was before the accident after all), making an orange pile back there on the concrete like someone had just smashed a pumpkin. Halloween and first year university costume parties, what fun. I took off my fisherman's vest and threw it down over the vomit, ashamed, and then, trudging home in my hip waders, thought of the poor Sobey's front end clerk who'd have to spray it all down the drain in the morning.

And that's how her and Martin began for me: with a fizzy orange puddle of upchuck, and the aforementioned weeping all the way back to the apartment, and an outfit you may have worn, dear Lee, sometime back in the good ol' days when the wilderness of Newfoundland opened up before you like the thighs of some real keen freshman English student.

POEM THREE OF TEN FOR AND ABOUT CATHERINE PRINCE

ROBOT VOICE

I don't know how many I've seen with it. Too many, to be honest.
Bad art videos wherein ROBOT VOICE addresses alienation, subjectivity
    blah blah.
See, it means that we're robots. You and me, Lee.
How it's hard to feel things anymore or something.
ROBOT VOICE going on and on over shots of some seaside cliffs
Or otherwise a scene of natural beauty, you know?
Where I'm guessing you get a sense of awe,
But really what you get to know
Is just how programmed your response to the footage is.

As far as I'm concerned, it's cliché.
But sometimes, like that night for instance,
Walking out of that parking lot by the mall
Back home to the apartment
ROBOT VOICE thundered in my head
As just another way of distancing myself
From the awful thought
Of that cab pulling away from the curb.

———— • ————

But later even still, months later, in fact, when it became apparent that this troll of Catherine's was more than just some random thing, more than a flavour of the week, was something other than a one-nighter, a quick fuck and a see you later (Catherine still claims, somehow, to this day, that she's never really *had* a one-night stand, by which she means, through some demented logic, that fucking someone any given night, and then again in the morning negates the "one-nightedness" of the thing (or, in a similar vein (as it were), a ten minute fuck in a bathroom doesn't count, given that she doesn't *actually* spend the night with said fuckee (as opposed to fuck-*er*, that is to say: Catherine) or further, how, given the nature of life as a sexually adventurous polyamorous Whatever, given how long and unpredictable life is (see accidents: car and/or plane), what may well appear in her sexual history to be a one-night stand remains open: there remains the possibility of a second night or even a third ha ha, thereby negating said "one-nightedness" once again and thereby leaving the slate (classroom or roadside) unsullied, as it were. That is to say: Free. Of muck. That is: in the former case, to torture this metaphor further: excretions, vaginal and/or penal, or, in the latter case: brain matter, intestinal blood, connective tissue, et cetera (Look, I'm sorry, okay?). In short, she may fuck the same dude in the future, so the book (sorry) is not yet closed on that (and I'm leaving out what she refers to as The Booty Call, which, for some reason, falls into a different category than one-night stand altogether (and also: Catherine's resistance to what may be termed "slutty" behaviour here runs counter to her sexual bravado, would seem to contradict her refusal to be "slut-shamed" et cetera, but nevertheless, is explained away by her claiming (as punk, feminist, anarchist), that she finds contradiction to be a fruitful place politically for exploration, subversion, and self-criticality blah blah)))), they invited me to the first of what would become many of their notorious "parties."

My dad always talked about hope, dear Lee. Speaking in terms of the labour movement, or the social justice movement, the movement for equality (my bowels ache with the thought of all this movement), he'd say that hope was the thing that kept you going. Even when everything is shit, the hope of a better future energizes the masses.

So it was hope—the loss of?—that was on my mind at that wretched, first "swinger" party at Martin's condo, a spacious three-bedroom affair with a glorious seaside view, heated floors and a balcony over which you looked and watched the glowing shapes of seagulls in the evening air diving and eating the shit that got pumped into the harbour and which (the condo, not the shit) was paid for by Mom and Dad.

Martin, the son of a big shot architect, the nephew of an Oxford educated lawyer who helped draw up the most repressive anti-union legislation in the country's history, was holding forth (without irony, I might add) about how he'd always been on the side of the underdog, the downtrodden, the losers, the unwashed—standing up to those bullies (that is, Canada, I guess)—and somehow not causing the room full of people around him to descend into convulsive fits of uncontrollable laughter. Who *are* these people? I asked myself, as hope—hope for anything, everything—began to slip away.

> Write book.
> Finish book.
> Book does well.
> Become a wunderkind.
> Attain happiness.

A porcelain gravy boat of coke sat on the glass coffee table.

The hot blonde I clocked upon arriving—a face that was, no joke, San Francisco 1969—pure, free, tanned, young. I stared at her and she at me.

Lee.

I.

Am.

Scared.

Shitless.

Catherine says, "Jesus, Joe, my entire head is numb. That coke is like, TERRIFFFFF."

The hot blonde now in front of me with a straw and a hand mirror.

"You vahnt?" she says.

Good God, she's like, Dutch, I think.

"Wha—wha—wha," I say.

"Joe's a drinker," Catherine says, putting her hand on the hot blonde's neck. "Fetch him a bourbon."

And while she's gone to do so, I see it, Lee. I see the light, you know?

I see the dawn, the burning head of the sun crowning on the horizon line.

There's this thing that keeps drawing my gaze.

There's like this beautiful thing happening.

And don't I hate it.

It isn't the hot blonde (I hear the lone ice cube rattle in the glass she's getting for me).

It is, dear Lee, dear God, dear doctor: Martin.

IT IS MARTIN.

Pudgy, flat-footed, short, a lazy eye.

There is just something about this guy, and I'm watching it happen right now.

He's sexy, that's what it is.

His hair is perfect.

And I hate him.

There's just no comparison here, Lee.

I look like a young Sam Shepard, and this guy is Groucho Marx with a beard (Karl?).

I'm Jackson Pollock, and he's some nobody who can't paint.

Me: Kurt. Him: Dave Grohl.

Me: Manet. Him: Meissonier.

Me: Nabokov. Him: Like, whoever is the shittiest writer in the world

(That is: Me?).

Me: Iggy. Him: An illiterate version of Lester Bangs.

He's just standing there, talking to someone. I mean, he's not even really doing anything, and yet, I see it, you know?

There's just something about the way he's holding that wineglass.

Something about the way his shoulders look in that sweater vest he's wearing.

He just doesn't seem to care.

He's just so, so confident.

He's cool.

He's cool in a way that no one I'd ever seen had been before. It isn't just that he wasn't trying, it's that even the thought of trying, the notion of considering what others may think was just so obviously not a thing that had ever, or would ever, occur to him.

"Yah, goot," my Dutch heroine says. She looks like Nico. Not the real one, but the actress from the Doors movie. The one that sucks Morrison off in the elevator.

I've just come on her tits in one of the bedrooms while some cute black girl rubbed away at herself on a chair in the corner watching us.

It's like Orgy Night at the United Nations.

"Yah, goot, bay-bee," she says, patting my behind.

This is the most dreadful party to which I've ever been.

And here's why:

Coming out into the living room again, here's, like, the Manson Family sprawled out on the floor and the chesterfield, except, it's not the Manson Family, it's just Martin and Catherine with some other chick, a few dudes sitting there, and they're talking.

Catherine is massaging Martin's foot.

His *foot*!

The men are twice Martin's age. I notice now just how deferential the older men are to him. Meanwhile, older men make me feel like I'm about fifteen years old.

(Grade Ten at Heart. 1990. I am fifteen years old. Martin is my age and yet Martin is also my dad. Grade Ten: MacBeth (GoD, in 1994, pinkie finger pointing skyward in the fascist salute, with his miniature glass of port, would've said: The Scottish Play).

> The dudes are raping and pillaging:
> Boy says: *Foul stack-headed villain!*
> Dude says: *What, you egg!* (runs boy through).
> Boy: *He has killed me, Mother!*
> And the baby, dear Lee, from the womb untimely ripped.
> (O Doctor, please help.))

Martin's in the middle of saying, "Desire *is* the revolution."

I clear my throat.

They see me.

There's a very distinct cult vibe in the room. Martin laying out how they need to bomb the Pentagon or something and then the sex aliens will rescue us all, you know? The pervy Anunnaki will come down in big spaceships shaped like glowing blue and purple pussies or something, I don't know.

"Thanks for the party," I say.

I grab my coat off a hook by the door.

I need to get away from the Branch Davidians, to get away from Martin, but even when I get away from the party, I know that Martin is going to follow me.

Even when I was balls-deep, as it were, with the Dutch girl in the bedroom, I was thinking about Martin, about how there was no way I could compete with him. The absolute certainty of this sent a finger of ice right into the Down Below.

Martin comes over to the door to see me off. He's stark naked, but despite this, I'm actually charmed. He's like the most charming garden gnome you've ever met.

"I'm really glad you could make it," his hand is warm and dry. "We want you around," he says, like Joey Ramone, and I'm out the door and down the elevator, and out onto the street and walking, Lee, all the way through the miserable town until I'm home.

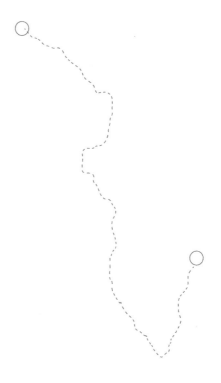

DAY. TWO.

Heart's Content to Gander

Be more normal.

When someone in the workplace asks how you are doing, say,
  "Fine, thank you, and you?" Do not deviate from this.

Do not deviate.

Enjoy life.

Do not deviate from this.

Visit artists' studios.

Encourage and cajole artists.

Attempt to appear interested in artists.

Ask questions pertaining to artists' art practice.

Tell artists you'll get back to them.

At first I thought it was your run of the mill case of Itchy Bum. I looked
it up online somewhere. Itchy Bum: something that just happens to you.
Kaboom, that's it.

"Honey," Catherine tells me. "Rub honey on your ass. It's a cure-all."

"I find that very unlikely."

"You know about bees?" She's already halfway through bottle
what?—four?—of the Carlo Rossi. "That dance they have?" Her eyes
scanning the road before us. Bright bugs appear and then are gone in
the blue air.

She tugs my sleeve. Right here next to me, the oldest friend I've ever
had. She's looking at me too seriously. "Do you know how they discovered
the secret language of bees?"

In that moment before you died, dear Lee, your bush plane driving headlong into the Labrador wilderness, you must have felt as though that final landscape and everything that had led you there was some dream playing out before your weeping eyes.

What were your final words?

Shit?

Fuck?

Oh, no?

To and fro, to and fro?

Catherine pulls some paper out of her purse, hands it to me.

"I want you to read something," she says. "I think it's for the new book, but I'm not sure."

I look at the front page.

I am seriously about to weep.

She hasn't asked me to read anything of hers for years.

"Just have a look," she says. "Honestly, you have no idea the pressure I'm under."

The car speeds up—her fists tighten on the wheel.

It goes like this:

The Bees and Eddie Cochrane

The old bird finally kicked it. Mom called that morning with the news, saying Nan had gotten through until the morning. Until the sun came up.

I had been there alone in the palliative care unit with Nan for a few hours the day before and knew it wouldn't be long. But I won't talk about that right now. Let's just say I held her hand the whole time, just like you might see in some Hollywood tear-jerker.

But I didn't cry or anything like that when Mom called with the news. I asked her if there was anything I could do.

"No," she said. "There's nothing for anyone to do."

She cried a little and then hung up. I put on a pot of coffee and waited for Lucy to wake up.

On Lucy's right shoulder and running down to the elbow there's a tattoo in plain black ink. It's a simple drawing that depicts the waggle dance bees do when they communicate. There's a series of dashes running down her arm that shows where the bees' footprints are. You know about this? Apparently, the scout bees have this elaborate way of communicating that looks like they're dancing. They move their legs in this way, and make sounds, and wiggle around to let the other bees know about where the nectar is. It's this kind of language they have, and back in the day, a bunch of scientists studied them in order to figure out something about how the hive goes about its business. I'm no expert, and Lucy could tell it better than me, but these scientists, they tried testing the limits of this language. This one scientist put a dish of sugar-water solution out for some bees from a nearby hive to find, and then moved it a little further away each day. The bees caught on to this pretty quick, until the scientist put the dish onto a boat moored out in the middle of some close-by lake. Then the scout bees couldn't convince their compatriots to go where the loot was, no matter how vigorously they danced. And according to Lucy, they danced their asses off, but none of the other workers would go because they knew nectar couldn't be located out in the middle of a lake. The scientists say this proved not only that the bees' dance was extremely detailed and sophisticated, but that they had an extremely good knowledge of the environment around the hive.

I like this tattoo because that was how I first met Lucy. It was back when I was bartending and she'd always come in with her boyfriend. She was wearing this sleeveless number the first time I ever saw her. A black cocktail dress, and I had been looking for any excuse to talk to her, so when I saw the tattoo I had to ask about it. When she told me about the bees' dance, I knew that she was really something special. Not just another pretty, long-necked girl hanging around with a balloon for a head and some gangster for a boyfriend. Not a girl with "The Beautiful Life" tattooed in Sanskrit above her ass.

So months later, after the boyfriend was off the scene and she'd come into the bar alone and I'd closed the place and we were having a drink after hours, I asked her to tell me about the scientists and the bees again. When she finished, she said, "Don't you think that's a cool thing to think about?"

"Yes," I said, "I do."

We kissed.

I took the car to the church with a friend of Mom's. This guy Mike who I guess has been in love with Mom for years since the divorce. This really nice, pudgy, red-headed guy with bad breath. At the funeral home he kept putting his arm around me and leaning in, saying, "Your Mom really is a very strong woman, but she needs you right now, Frankie." Me trying not to think about whatever must be going on with his gums to make his breath that way. Me at the funeral home with a bunch of vaguely familiar relatives, shuffling around with photos of Nan in 1941 as a backdrop, and the urn there on a plinth framed by a truckload of flowers.

So anyway, we drive out to the church and the whole time he's trying to console me. Don't get me wrong, here, okay? It was nice of him, but he was just talking too much, and Lucy was in the backseat biting her fingernails, probably freaking out about what we had to do that day. But there's a stretch where he doesn't say anything, and neither do I, driving through the subdivisions and strip malls that make up St. John's, and finally I say, "Man, can we listen to some music?" Because even worse than Mike's nattering is the sound of the wind coming through his open window, the sound of everything just rushing past us, we're barrelling down that road, you know? And I'm so fucked up I don't even really remember where the church is. For a second there I really have no idea where we're going. It all just seems very unfamiliar and strange to me. Like the town where I grew up is suddenly a blank page. Like even though Mike knows the way and the right turns to make, I don't, and there's this feeling akin to what I can only assume being blind is like: I just trust in Mike that we're headed the right way even though it feels like at every stoplight and crosswalk, I don't know where we're going.

Past the Wendy's, the McDonald's, the Burger King, the car dealership, the Chapters. Past the mall, the Western Union, Cash Converters, the Keg, I fumble for the binder of CDs and pull out, written in scrawled magic marker, what appears to be an Eddie Cochrane album.

See, Mike volunteers at the local university radio station, where he plays all this old stuff every Sunday morning at something ridiculous like 5 AM So it's Eddie Cochrane and Gene Vincent kind of stuff amongst a slew of others I couldn't attempt to name. But Mom would get up early sometimes and listen to his show, especially lately, saying, "I find it comforting to start the day that way." His voice coming over the airwaves to find Mom in her nightgown, with a cup of tea, waiting for Nan to die.

And we pull into the parking lot of the church finally with Cochrane's *Summertime Blues* blaring through the speakers and it's a beautiful day. There are some people on the steps of the church, and I see Mom and a couple of my uncles and my aunt standing around and a few cousins and I suddenly realize how hot the day is, and how I'm probably going to sweat through this blazer in about five seconds, given how shiny everyone's faces are.

"Francis," Mom says as Lucy and I come up the steps. She hugs me.

"How are you?" I ask casually, and then think what a dumb fuck I am for asking it. I take the blazer off and see there are already dark circles under my armpits.

"Hi Lucy." Mom takes hold of her hand. She scans Lucy's arm where the bees are inscribed. She's always thought only criminals got tattoos, and could never understand how popular they'd become.

We go into the great hollow vault of the church and take our seats right up in front there, where the coffin is gleaming like a brand new car on the centre of the altar. Eddie Cochrane and Gene Vincent were in a car accident together, did you know that? This was back in 1960, around the time my grandfather was in jail for passing rubber cheques. That was how Cochrane died, but I only know about it through another dead musician whose interviews I watch on YouTube after Lucy's gone to bed. They crashed right into a light post and Cochrane flew through that windshield and died later in an English hospital.

And Gene Vincent had a limp for the rest of his life after that accident. I guess that would be a pretty awful thing: every step reminding you of that pal you had who died maybe because you were driving too fast, and maybe you'd been drinking or something.

And just then, the organ starts and we all stand up and something really horrible happens. The priest is there on the altar behind the podium, and I see for the first time these two ladies up there with him. Church volunteers, I guess. There's this one lady who looks just like some emaciated Tammy Faye Bakker, and when Lucy sees her, we just start giggling. I mean, it's horrible, but this lady's face is just like some mask. It's like some powder bomb went off, covering her cheeks and forehead, and her eyes plastered in this blue eyeshadow and she just looks like a wreck, to be honest. And Lucy and I, standing there in the first row, just can't stop laughing, stupidly, and for no apparent reason at all.

So maybe Mom noticed, or maybe not, but Lucy had to take me out of the church even before everyone had finished the hymn. There was just something about that woman's face I couldn't handle, you know?

Outside on the steps of the church, I felt much better, but I sure couldn't go back inside there, not for anything in the world. And I looked at Lucy then, she had her arms around me. My face felt wet. In the air, we heard the music seeping out through the doors behind us. There was some silent language around us, and I thought I could understand the bees Lucy has tattooed on her shoulder. And I know, that even here, now, telling you this, it's impossible for you to know what I'm trying to say.

I feel Catherine's eyes on me as I get to the last page, and say nothing for a minute, dizzy from reading with the car moving.

I wasn't in town when her Mom died.

I was in transit—mid-flight from Toronto to home because Catherine had called to tell me it wouldn't be long.

Three hours rereading about all the sights of Newfoundland in a glossy magazine.

Just a block of words on the page.

All the dead bodies under the ground.

For some reason, I'm worried I said something out loud and gave away how morose and fucked up I am to Catherine.

I look over at her and try to figure out what she'd like me to say.

"That's some awesome shit."

It didn't come out right. A little too official sounding, but she grins at me anyway. She appreciates the effort.

—— • ——

We drive now away from the ocean inland toward the heart of the island. The gravel shoulders of the highway giving way to ditches either side of us, and beyond the ditches, the shrubbery and then the thin trees and further back beyond the thin trees, the rolling hills, big grey stones in moss, still pools of dead water, marshlands, reeds, tall grass and in the distance further still, sunlight shining on the windows of cars moving in a town beyond.

Here and there, ramshackle houses, bare clapboard beneath chipped paint, black and brown shingles edged with green moss dislodged from the roofs. Discarded toys, car parts strewn in the grass, whirligigs, front yard gardens overgrown and neglected. Others kept up. Neat rectangles impossibly green. New ATVs in the driveways. Satellite dishes, laundry lines, lobster traps as garden decoration, and yes, Lee, kids playing in the front of these houses. Once, an astonishing red kite in the blue sky.

In the valley a half hour from town, the ocean on one side, and here, on the left, great grey boulders left scattershot in the shadow of one enormous hill. The huge wide open sky above our heads and the cool dark shadows beside us and as the car moves on, the sun coming down red and bloody ahead of us, the evening air red and the dust in the car's wake a red cloud in the slanted beams of that sun descending now toward the horizon as behind us—I see it in the side-view mirror of the Crown Royal—a pale sliver of moon like a silver hook in the sky and the metal and plastic and leather and glass of the car hurtling through space, a silver comet through red haze, a coffin shot out from some distant space station in orbit around some lonely dead star and I'm struck by the power and silence of the engine which is like some terrible pounding heart of heat and grease and metal dragging us onward over the grey, winding road before us, onward onward into what and where who knows, dear Lee.

Roadside signs offering root vegetables, cod and meat, fishnet repair, carpentry and labour. Buoys painted bright red and yellow. Plywood renderings of Snow White and Sleeping Beauty done slap-dash in peeling exterior house paint, their crudely rendered faces watch us as we pass.

The horizon line a long red wound, and here, Catherine takes a right down a dirt lane I didn't see, over rocks and potholes, brown puddles of still water, through the blue overhang of elms, white birch, down further into some unknown valley, where at the bottom, a tiny clapboard house awaits us, the tarpaper roof sunken in, the yard out front with a million discarded, hand carved foxes, squirrels, dogs, crows, seagulls, hawks. A rusted swing set with the seats missing, the chains hanging limply down to the ground. A chimney with its white smoke floating up into the first bright stars which have appeared above our heads.

Catherine kills the engine and looks at me.

"Surprise," she says.

A slight man of sixty-five years, Harry Sullivan, cut from wood. Which is to say, dear Lee, hands and face dark brown and craggy, the fingernails too long, the edges yellowed crescent moons.

It's an artist studio, but he calls it his shed. Moths bump their blunt heads on the dirty glass of the lone window. Around back of the house he leads us with an antique lantern's beam on the wet grass, saying, I has these dreams, and then I makes the dreams real. I sees the thing in my head. Animals. And then I chops them out of the wood. All kinds of wood around. Var, birch. I cuts the dream out.

I thought he was dead.

No one at the gallery has heard anything about him in years and years. Down in the archives, I found a catalogue with images of his work from some show in the mid-nineties, before the government moved everything to the ultra-modern location that I now call my place of work.

A two-headed cat. A pig with wings. Feral, emaciated white rabbits with fangs sharp as razor wire. A deranged fisherman with a bloody knife.

Peggy was dismissive when I brought him up at the gallery's programming meeting.

"That crackpot?" she said. "No thanks. That isn't the sort of thing we support here. And besides, he died or maybe he's in the mental."

But somehow, Catherine has found him. This is her gift to me. Having had to listen to me for so many years complain about the locals, this is her way of saying, Look, this old loon is surviving in the desert. So can you.

She's smiling now as Harry unlatches the door to the shed, and inside, he shows us this painting he's been working on, he says, though he's hardly painted anything before.

He shines the light, the moths tapping the windowpane, and there on a makeshift workbench is the latest creation: a big beautiful, glorious, Newfoundland landscape: ocean, cliffs, blue sky, white clouds, and there, above it all, a giant white ass in the sky above some unknowing, smiling figure, a giant load of shit descending from the ass down onto the figure's head.

We laugh. So does he.

"It's called God Shits on My Head," he says. "One reason you should always wear a hat. To keep God from shitting on you."

He nods at me. A deferential little dip of the head. He's wearing a red toque with a giant pompom.

Catherine and I laugh again. This is some funny shit.

Harry nods and smiles. Gaps in his teeth like you wouldn't believe.

And now he leads us through the dark woods surrounding his shack. The lone beam of the lantern white on the grass and white on the trunks and branches of the trees. Carved animals crouch beside logs: the feral rabbits' eyes agleam, a bright blue dog on the verge of running. Stumbling over roots, sink holes, stones in the path, in a clearing Harry Sullivan has carved a full-on re-creation of the Last Supper.

But the best piece, he says, is something you can't see.

We're standing in a field close by to his house, I can see the smoke from the nearby chimney hanging thickly in the air, when Harry Sullivan spreads his arms out in the moonlight before us—in the dark, swaying in the slight breeze, many hundreds of lupin flowers.

"See, I carved a bunch of these little skeletons from wood," he says. "Like, baby skeletons and some adult-sized skeletons. And I buried them all here in a mass grave."

But you wouldn't know it by looking—only the flowers cover the ground where Harry is gesturing, so it must have been years ago that he'd done it—and no one would ever know, seemingly, unless Harry was there to tell you.

"I was thinking about trauma," Harry says. "In each skull, I put a seed. With a hole in each skull through which the seed would grow."

Each seed, a bullet.

I think of that old fascist song from the Falange in Spain during the war: *I'm going to kill more Reds than there are flowers in May and June.*

Later, at the fold-out card table in his kitchen, I ask him about it.

"You see all these people here, visiting us from all over the world—it's such a beautiful place, Newfoundland—and what they don't know is that beneath the very ground they're on are so many mass graves, so many bodies—they're everywhere—but I believe that the trauma of the past comes to us through the dead and through the land. That the dead communicate with us in a way that we can't even really perceive—from a past we won't allow ourselves to remember."

Catherine watching us so closely, rolling her cigarette, as the wood in the wood stove cracks and burns.

She slams back the rest of the rum and coke Harry had fixed for her.

"It's time to go, Joe," she says, lighting up.

I watch the little flame of her match as she blows it out.

—— • ——

Observe beauty.

Feel it. I mean, really feel it.

Continue to observe beauty and continue to feel it.

Tell someone about it.

Realize communicating your experience of beauty makes you and
others feel less alone in the world.

Understand people.

Understand social situations with more clarity and confidence.

React with subtlety and grace.

React with good humour.

Be someone who sets people at ease.

Be more charming.

Despite how handsome you are, feign modesty.

Pretend to be oblivious to boobs, bums, eyelashes, recent art school
graduates, Catherine.

Pretend to be shy, yet be funny when possible. Quietly, of course.

Pay attention to what people say, their moods, etc.,

On the highway again, I'm thinking about what Harry said about
trauma—all those bodies under the ground—and of how, after I'd first
arrived in Spain, I watched fat tourists sunbathing at the beach and could
think of nothing but the bones of the dead under all that beautiful sand,
under the beautiful hills and the trees and the scorching earth.

And, for some reason, me and Catherine silent as the car speeds
along—the dead and the trauma of the past maybe numbing us—
I remember watching Michel Foucault swirl the ice in his scotch at a
party years before.

I feel bad for even thinking that, because it wasn't Michel Foucault,
it was Ryan Ryan, the owner of the local publishing house—*An agent
provocateur for change* is its tagline—but Ryan looks just like Foucault. He's
showing me the ledgers from the long history of his family's business
in St. John's. Me and him in one of the many bedrooms of his mansion
with a dozen of these leather-bound tomes on a mahogany desk next to

a window which looks out through the trees at the Narrows where I see the lighthouse beam from Cape Spear sweep across the banks of fog.

Another party, another round of introductions. Catherine has just become known to the cultural gatekeepers, as she calls them. Catherine having told Ryan about my Lee Wulff obsession—which he must have misunderstood somehow because he says, "I was thinking about donating something to the provincial archives. Maybe you'd have a look?"

So here we are—Ryan's family, the, like, richest clan of merchants around, and the oldest—the ledgers with dates stretching back to the 1700s—and everywhere on the walls of this ancestral home, those creepy daguerreotype photos of his forefathers staring menacingly and so full of contempt out from their elaborate gilt frames.

Fish, wool, rope and tinder. Coal, burlap, fur, blubber.

Ammunition, blankets.

The writing is almost illegible, but I can make most of it out. The yellow and brown pages smell like dust.

"They're remarkable," I say, but the truth is I'm a little bored by them. Disappointed it's not something about you, Lee, yet also pleased that someone like Ryan would even think to share this with me.

"You should see some of the old journals and diaries," he says. "In some ways, things change so little."

"I think the archives would be thrilled to have them," I say, which isn't a lie—the archives are filled with this junk, and Ryan flips the cover of the ledger closed.

His hand brushes mine as he collects the books and stacks them on the bedside table.

"My great great grandmother was a real spitfire. A feminist. And a dyke, as it turns out."

I don't know quite what to say—it's usually the sort of thing I'd think was cool. I can hear the party picking up downstairs, the people's voices rising up to us through the carpeted floor.

"Wanna rail?" he says.

For a second I think this is his weird way of asking me to fuck, but that can't be right. There's tense silence as I try to figure out what he means.

He crosses the room toward me, eyes locked on mine, digging in his pocket.

"Loves and hates and passions," he says, taking out a little plastic bag. He holds it up between his index finger and thumb for me to see. I wonder, in the name of God, from where, oh where, does all the cocaine come.

"We're respectable now, but back then, my people were common criminals. Intimidation, extortion, smuggling, you name it." He does up a couple of fat lines on the desk. "After you," he says, gesturing toward them, then continuing—"Kidnapping and murder, no doubt. All sorts of skullduggery."

I hesitate. I'd never tried cocaine, and I was thinking about how maybe Ryan's great great grandfather once sat at this very desk, plotting the ruin by any means of the French, the indigenous population, leftists, enemies not yet even born, anyone.

I bend at the waist with Ryan's offered straw in my nose, hoping I'm doing it right, my head coming down to the desk where the reflection of his belt buckle gleams on the surface of the wood.

I snort it. My sinuses clear.

There's this burning sensation that gives way to pleasant tingling in my brain.

"Atta boy," he says. "Oh dear, what a mess."

He wipes my nostrils with his fingers, and they linger a moment on my lips.

I watch him bend to take his turn.

"Skullduggery," he smiles. "What a fantastic word."

He's wearing grey trousers, a white turtleneck, a blue sport coat with gold buttons agleam—I am the captain of this ship—and agleam is the great bald head, the many gold rings upon Ryan's fingers, the lenses of his eyeglasses in the light of the nearby fire which burns in the hearth of his living room.

"How long have you and Catherine been together, John," he's asking.

"It's Joe," I say, which I've already told him—twice—but he's not listening. He's distracted by a couple of his other guests on the chesterfield next to us—"Our downtown rental property has tripled in value over the last year."—and my gaze comes to the fire, its heat making me sweat.

I'm totally stoned. It takes all of my willpower to not grind my teeth. I'm worried everyone knows I'm stoned. Which must mean I'm not that stoned. So I relax, at which point, I start grinding my teeth.

Catherine bursts into the room, spilling her wine—it's how I know she's playing it up. I've never seen her spill a drink in her entire life.

"Fuck, man, the cramps are killing me," she says, and everyone stops talking. I realize the whole time we've been here, a cool-jazz record has been playing. Chet Baker singing in the background. Catherine puts her hand on her abdomen.

She looks at Ryan.

"Ever try waiting tables while you're on the rag" she asks him. "It's hell on earth. Everything's hell on earth when you're on the rag."

She throws a glance around the room.

I look at the painting above the mantle. One of the local painters in imitation of Renoir. A preteen ballerina on points in a gloomy rehearsal studio, a bouquet of roses held in her hands over her pelvis.

Ryan examines the toe of his shoe, and I do likewise. White, 1970s loafers to match the turtleneck.

"It's a fucking waterfall," Catherine says, spilling more wine on the rug. She puts her half-full glass on the floor. Takes her tobacco from her purse. Kicks the glass over. Rolls a cigarette.

From a pocket, Ryan produces a white handkerchief, and is on his knees at Catherine's feet, soaking up the red stain.

She's looking down at his bald head, the only sounds a pop from the fireplace, Chet Baker saying, You make me smile with my heart.

She licks the cigarette slowly, and then, more slowly, puts it between her lips. Lights it with a red cigarette lighter. Smoke curls up.

"Would you mind taking that outside," says Ryan.

She blows smoke.

"Sorry," she says, smiling, looking down again—then at me, winking. "Come on, Joe, let's split." She flicks the cigarette into the fire, and, waving like the queen, says, "Thanks for the pawty."

I get up to follow her, and look at Ryan where he's kneeling on the floor. Someone helps him to his feet.

Something about watching him there, reminds me of my dad.

But then Catherine takes my hand, and we are out the door and on our way to her place.

"Trawsh. So much trawsh. My toxes paid your way here, dawling," she's saying in the mock-voice of the party guests, later, at the tiny apartment she's rented above the video store and the rub and tug—this is before she's moved in with Martin.

"Ah, dawling, that pawty was *dread*ful. Honestly, dawling—such trawsh."

She's really drunk now—hands steady as a heartbeat. We're laying on the bed. One of her legs hangs off the bed onto the floor, the other draped over me.

"Did you have a good time?" I say.

I'm not talking about the party.

"An agent provocateur for change," she spits. "Ever notice how it's the rich white dudes who're the first to claim outlaw status? Rebels—fuck 'em. Or at least fuck the people posing as rebels. My mother was more rebellious than any writer I've ever met."

I laugh. She glares at me.

"I'm serious," she says. "Fat, poor and uneducated when the whole world tells you to be thin and rich and clean and happy. Mom didn't have much time to worry about happiness—she was too busy working."

"Yeah, but Ryan is only talking about artistic change. It's not societal."

She rips a loud one.

"That's exactly my point. But his tagline is ambiguous. It's the cachet of dissent without the dissent."

What a stink.

"He's not so bad," I say.

Catherine lays her glass of wine on the bedside milk crate. She changes the CD in the player. For sex, it was *Fun House*. For afterward, it's *Nevermind*.

"If every rich boy in the universe claims to be a rebel, then how do you rebel from *that*?"

She hits play on the player.

"I guess that's what we're trying to figure out," I say.

We listen to the first few songs on the album.

So much rage and sadness and humour.

Followed shortly thereafter by disillusionment.

I remember when that album came out, it was like someone was speaking directly to me. Someone else saw how cheesy and shitty and boring everything was. Someone saw how corrupt everything was.

We weren't alone—and then every preppy jock at Heart became a Nirvana fan.

When Kurt Cobain shot himself, I realized how perfect his life and art were. How could things turn out any differently than they did? *Nevermind* cozying up to Poison, Motley Crue and Aerosmith in the CD collection of a million future date rapists.

Given a choice between that, and a bullet, I'd take the bullet every time.

"Look—I kinda wanna sleep alone tonight," she says.

She's staring up at the ceiling, chewing her lip.

It's the night before the very first SCUM meeting. She wants to be ready.

"Okay," I say.

I get dressed in front of her, looking down at the floor.

"You mad?" she says.

"Of course not," I say, yanking up my underwear.

I close the door without a sound and lock it with the key she's given me. The music turns off before I'm even down the stairs.

POEM FOUR OF TEN FOR AND ABOUT CATHERINE PRINCE

ANTHRAX

Because I was one of those smart kids
I looked it up,
asked my dad about it.
Something cows get,
he told me,
but also
one kick-ass thrash band.
And much later,
something you sent in the mail
to fuck shit up.
Me wearing an Anthrax Judge Dredd t-shirt
a speech balloon
in which he said: Mosh It Up.
A tent of black cotton
because I was one skinny little wisp
who read too many comic books
Catherine picking me out from the herd
in that creative writing class
because it looked like I was smothering in that thing
(the shirt or the class itself, I don't know).
But also because
Little Joe Penny
wrote like dynamite,
like a Marshall stack exploding
on the stage of some metal fest
where your eardrums pop and you're just as likely
to get a boot to the head
at the front of the stage,

a billy club smack from security,
as anything else.
And afterwards you sport that shiner or bruise
with as much pride as Dredd does
his badge,
and you think about yourself:
Don't Fuck With Me.

—— • ——

Jess spoons my back, and in front, as I lay on my side, I wrap the baby in my arms. That's the only way I can sleep, but it's not Jess and the baby, of course, it's just a couple of pillows I arrange that way. And anyway, those pillows suck because they'd been washed recently, they smelled too clean, so I might as well have been wrapping my arms around one of Martin's marshmallows.

The marshmallows came earlier. Catherine and Martin, a rented cabin, the three of us down at the beach sitting around a fire.

"You're suffering from Stockholm Syndrome," I'd said to her, right in front of Martin.

They'd been talking about a property Martin was thinking of buying.

"Jesus Christ, Joe-Joe. Be nice."

"It's true." I looked at that charming little engineer over the flames.

"Maybe I should go," he said.

He got up and padded down to where the tide came up to the sand.

"What the fuck is wrong with you?" Catherine said.

"Just cause the prison is well decorated doesn't make it any less of one."

"You're such a drama queen. And you really have no idea."

"At least I'm not a fool."

"Fuck sakes. This was Martin's idea, you know. Bringing you out here."

"Yeah, well, I can't be bought. Not like some."

She stood up suddenly. I was thinking, I'm about to get a patented left hook.

She hissed at me.

"Martin is somebody who could probably understand what the fuck you're going through."

"Well, sorry," I said.

I flicked a twig into the fire.

She stomped off down to the water.

Her and Martin looking out at the moon.

I left them to it—the fire, the moon, the sand, the beach, the water. Up through the woods, a path lit dimly.

Back to the cabin, where I sat on the front deck in a lawn chair looking at nothing in particular. Before long, Martin showed up alone.

"Look, sorry about that," I said.

"It's all right. Here," he held out his hand, and therein, dear Lee, in that soft pink palm of his, the peace offering. A marshmallow. I popped it into my mouth.

"I'm gonna turn in for the night," he said.

"Cool."

"Good night."

I waited a few minutes and then I went into my room and got into bed.

Catherine came back. I heard the front door of the cabin. Her boots dropped to the floor, one, two. The fridge door opened. Then it closed.

I heard her and Martin murmuring to each other through the thin wall.

And then I heard Catherine's little-girl laughter.

Lying there in the dark, listening to them.

Light in through the window making a grey rectangle on the wall.

The fresh smell of the sheets, those two pillows.

The old cabin creaking in its foundation.

I was thinking there must be some kind of lesson to be learned here, and there was—

> Stop having erections.
> Stop being greedy.
> Stop trying to be the Messiah.
> Be the Messiah.
> Continue to be greedy.

On the first anniversary of the accident, I baked a cake. Popped a single candle in the top and lit it while Catherine watched me, shaking her head.

At some point during the evening, Catherine excused herself and went into the bathroom to phone Martin. I stood out in the hall, eavesdropping. "He's fine. I mean, I think he's fine. He says he's fine. He's still on the medication at least."

Not that it was working—Doc Sparling with a new dosage every two weeks—and me going up down, up down—unable to get out of bed one day, on a rocket ship the next.

Freshly returned from that prolonged "holiday" in Spain, my body hard and brown and these thin arms scarred from the sharp branches of olive trees, I cut up a couple slices of cake for my best pal and me, and thought 'Viva la Muerte,' the rallying cry for Franco's men back when the shit show began and that brutal gang of murderers got things going with a carnival of rape and beheading and torture and you-name-it.

Viva la Muerte, I'd think, waiting for the bus, or at the mall, or when I signed the papers for the purchase of my first house. Viva la Muerte, hammering nails for raised beds in the backyard, buying seeds at the garden shop, walking to the corner store. Viva la Muerte, in my dreams, getting my hair cut, at the beach with Catherine and Martin that first summer after I'd returned, the sun on the water burning the eyes right out of my skull.

Happy Anniversary, every year it seems to come quicker than the last. You're here, you're gone, your eyes blink, dot-dash-dot, Hello, Goodbye, a signal sent out into the universe, to and fro, you move, you wait, you pace, you speak, you're silent, Happy Anniversary.

—— • ——

Here we are again plunging headlong. Here are the empty bottles of wine, the empty Sprite, I'm dozing, waking life interrupting my dreams. We were in love, Jess climbed into an empty mine shaft, that's what I thought. Her life an empty mine shaft and in the deep vault underneath she waited for the roof to cave in. She was waiting for the smothering weight of the entire world to come down. Yes, Lee, we were unhappy. Obvi. And she was driving away to who knows where. "Back to the civilized world," she had said, the hatchback packed with everything she owned.

The engine beneath this hood and the pistons working maniacally. The oil and grease of this machine throbbing beneath us. We are pitched headlong into nothingness. What scares you, Lee? Anything? Now that you've made the trip?

—— • ——

There's a clearing by some little-used salmon river way out back there where not even the Americans and their big dollars and expensive fly rods ever went. I read about it in *Bush Pilot Angler,* the book you wrote, Mr. Wulff, about discovering Newfoundland. Somewhere out there off the highway up the Western Coast I pictured myself building a fire, making bannock in a tin above the flames. I want to know more about these rivers than most anyone had forgotten, most anyone had forgotten almost, except for you, Lee Wulff, who could intuit and know and decipher and feel where the little parr fed and dreamed before finding their way out into the North Atlantic where their parents had bitten and fought and died and sank to the bottom of the sea.

Bottom feeders.

That's the salmon in their saltwater days.

That's them waiting for whatever rare, random descent of food makes its way down from the surface, or else upon some invisible underwater current, and that's just what I'll see, I imagine, in my lean-to built from fallen logs and a blue tarp light as a store-bought rod. That's just what I'll see, because Catherine says that after the festival, after the Dandelion, she's gonna take me off the beaten path to where you once lived, Lee Wulff. Because, then, Catherine says, I can put this book, this dreaded Bible of mine I keep in the top drawer of my office at the Gallery (and which right now lies in the trunk of this car), I can finally put this thing to bed and say goodnight to it, and can eventually put this hungry wandering spirit of mine to sleep at night in my warm bed without worrying anymore about what happened.

But I will not talk of Spain or my foolish reasons for going there. I will not mention how I traced the path of the Republican resistance during the Civil War. I won't mention the glint of my pick in the very dry ground at the foot of the Pyrenees, or anything otherwise about how sometimes I thought I could feel my heart being torn to bits upon the distant teeth of that mountain range, or of the snow upon the peaks of those mountains, or finally how I found my way back to Canada six months later, the entire trip having changed really nothing in the old Down Below, or for that matter, the Up Above, my mind still just a wreck of twisted metal, glass, asphalt and blood.

I will not talk of Spain—but I will talk about how it came to be that I went there.

After I'd checked myself into the hospital—I'd been there two weeks and had survived on a diet consisting mainly of ice cubes and sedatives—Catherine came to visit me.

"I've brought you something to read," she said, and I worried, seeing the shiny magazine in her hand, that it was another interview or review of hers that'd just come out or whatever—but it wasn't. It was the autumn issue of *Visual Art News*.

"When I saw this review I thought of you, Joe. Like, it's about Spain—the war in Spain. There's this show on and there's this review of it."

I had long before given up on reading anything of interest in the Canadian art critical press, but what else was I gonna do with my time?

After Catherine left, I flipped it open to where she had the page marked with a slip of paper.

What I was about to read forced me to book my flight a few months later to what had been the Republican zone.

> In 2003, I lived in Spain for four months, travelling from Barcelona to Malaga in the south. I'd just graduated from art school and felt like I was cracking up and that I needed to escape Halifax: everything in the world felt dead. I didn't know it at the time, but the experience

of living in Spain was the preliminary groundwork for a novel that will see publication in the fall of 2016—a novel that links personal trauma to large-scale international atrocities both contemporary and historical.

Last week, I took my one-year-old daughter to Eastern Edge Gallery in St. John's to see Coco Guzman's *Los Fantasmas/The Ghosts*— an exhibition of bright, highly detailed cartoon-like drawings linking the current political unrest in Spain to the brutality of the Spanish Civil War. The nineteen drawings draw the viewer across Spain in a manner that mimics the fascists' blood-thirsty march across the country. Beneath the ground, the forgotten victims of Franco's violence seek to make their presence known in the bright world above them—as contemporary conflicts abound at the sites of famous or little-known historical trauma, Guzman depicts how the blood or the residual energy from the bodies seeps upward into the light and conflict of today's Spain. There is no escaping the brutality of the past. I looked down at my daughter in her stroller and wondered how and when the fucked-up things that I'd done, or what my dad had done, or what my grandfather had done would play out in her life, and if there wasn't some way to reconcile it all. In my research of the civil war, I read that after the fascists passed through a town, killing or driving off every male of fighting age, they'd write on the public walls: YOUR WOMEN WILL GIVE BIRTH TO FASCISTS.

Everything, from the vegetation to the various geographical details specific to the places depicted, are imbued with this residual energy—the collective trauma of the past resides in the soil and in the fruit of the trees and the air and the water. Says Coco: "In my work, whether *Los Fantasmas* or other, I always try to visibilize what is made invisible or silent. I believe that secrets have a way to travel through the blood and the land, despite the fact that dominant society does its best to silence them."

In contemporary Madrid, mass popular protests against the state's so-called "austerity measures" are shown above the innumerable skeletons of Franco's victims. Police in riot gear—that unmistakable and pan-cultural symbol of domination—club protestors with their batons. From Coco's artist statement that accompanies the exhibition: "When the fascists sieged Madrid, the population hung anti-fascist banners all over the city. The courage of the population is now back. In a state of bankruptcy and daily anger, hundreds of thousands of people are taking the streets against new criminal policies. With 500 families evicted from their houses every day, daily suicides, 60% youth unemployment, 28% of total unemployment, new laws implemented by the Catholic church, a terrifying increase in sexism, racism and homophobia, institutional corruption, etc . . . Spanish people are finding new strategies of resistance."

In an email exchange with the artist, I just had one question:

Do you have hope for the future?

They[1] said:

Many people believe these drawings are sad. This took me by surprise the first time someone told this to me. I always thought the drawings to be a tribute to hope, even when it may need 80 years for values, ideas and politics to come out in the light again. I guess that for me, the past cannot be changed, and as sad as it is that so many people were killed I have no power about this. The power I have is to keep their memories alive and keep fighting for their values. I am hopeful and proud of the contemporary part of society in Spain that is bringing these values to live again. For me, Los Fantasmas *has always been a piece about hope and survival through silence and genocide. This is exactly what the last panel of the show depicts: a group of children discovering a mass grave*

---

[1] Coco's preferred pronoun is "they," used in the singular as a gender-neutral term.

and finding that under each neck, there was an empty bottle containing the name of the body. These bottles were put there by the relatives of the assassinated in the hope that one day the bodies will be unburied and they will receive a proper burial. And it happened, it took 80 years for these bodies to be buried properly, but it happened. If these families had hope, I cannot stop myself from having hope too.

After seeing the exhibition, we were outside Eastern Edge and the sun was beating down. I pushed Audrey in her stroller along the harbourfront, looking at the water. All around us the trees and the hills and the old battlements upon the hills where the flags of Canada and Newfoundland were bright in the air—and in the ground beneath, what were our own ghosts silently telling us?

—Craig Francis Power is an artist and writer from St. John's

—— • ——

This is how Catherine fucks you:

A quick, sharp, slap to the face. Catherine straddles you. Choking you. She thinks you're a fucking imbecile. She says—Know what? You're dumb as shit.

She could grind you into dust with that pelvis of hers. She's too intelligent for you. She's too everything for you. She fucks like a champion. She could teach all of your promiscuous pretty boy writers a thing or two, let me tell you. All the Byrons, and the Kerouacs, and Christ, I don't know, the Ted Hugheses blah blah blah, bowing down before her.

A dancer's body—muscles cut right out of marble. And look at you: gut like a jelly roll and hands soft as fuck.

In the three-way mirror in the hall, you stand behind her. You try to catch her eye. Her face in the reflection. She's not into it. You're there only as an object of her furious contempt. But once it does happen, you're holding her hair back from her face. She looks at you almost by accident.

You see that it's not the look you wanted, but something else—she's laughing at you. Somewhere behind that spark in her eyes.

And now, here she is on top of you. Full on into her period. Pounding you into submission. Bam bam bam bam. There's blood up to your throat. Bloody handprints on the wall. The sheets gone from white to pink to red like murder.

And then, after she comes—her lip curled in an Elvis Presley sneer—you think she's done with you? Uh-uh. Bite down on that pillow. The one your wife bought filled with goose down. You feel those feathers prick your gums through the fabric. Encore, maestro, encore. That laugh of hers as she spreads your ass cheeks. Brings the baton straight home—the end of Lonely Street—and your breath catches in your fish belly throat. A dildo as big and as black as the night sky, ha ha, you clichéd little shit.

And then, the best fuck of your life over and done with, what does my sweet Catherine do? She rolls a Drum. Puts it between her teeth. Lights that thing with a pair of paws just covered in gore, honey, because she can only come while she's playing with herself, especially given what she's just had to work with. And before you even know it, she's out your door. Down that lovely little manicured footpath. Stones you'd bought straight up from the local quarry, and on her way down your street. And for the next three days, you're so fuck-struck, your hands tremble so much, you worry about crashing the new Mercedes.

— • —

"They're making a film of *On the Road*," Catherine says. I'm watching the solid yellow line of the highway dance before us.

"Jesus Christ," I say. "Is nothing sacred?"

"Evidently not." Catherine shifts to fifth and her foot goes down. Swerve, shift, gear down gear up, pass, slow down, curse, light a cigarette, pass again and laugh.

"With that little bitch from *Twilight*, of all things. What's her name?"

"Those vampire movies?"

"Not that I needed any more proof, but the world's gone to shit."

"I always get them mixed up with the kids from *Harry Potter*."

"You spend too much time in your office," she says.

"And anyway," I say, "I thought you'd be in favour of that kind of stuff."

"What? The vampire girl?"

"Tearing down what came before," I say. We're moving to the top of a big hill. All around us, the barrens stretch out far as you can see.

"There are limits to everything, Joe. There's still such a thing as good taste."

We're coming down the other side of the hill. There isn't a single bird in the sky or anywhere else.

That word again. *Taste*. There's both good and bad. The M FA Curating taught me that, amongst what else, I'm not sure. But sometimes good taste is actually bad taste, and what's bad is good. Good being subversive. Rebellious, I guess. But good could also really be bad, even if subversive. And then there's bad taste, which is what used to be good taste. Paintings of flowers and skulls or something. Roses in empty wine bottles. And bad taste, kitsch, that's been good taste for a long time now, so much so that paintings of flowers and skulls might be good again. It's hard to say, really.

"Hey, you know where that witch on a broomstick thing comes from?" Catherine says. "Martin told me about it. Back in the day, these women would make their concoctions. Hallucinogens and what-not."

"Does this relate to the vampire thing?" I say.

"They would make this paste from, like, magic mushrooms," Catherine says, her tongue coming out and touching the point of an incisor.

"And then they'd apply the paste to a wooden dildo and put it home in the honey pot." Her smile broadens. "Imagine that. No wonder people wanted to burn those bitches. Getting stoned while masturbating? I could get into that."

"Or it could get into you," I say. That tongue comes out again, and she smiles at me.

That's how Catherine wants to be seen. Like one of those witch bitches riding a broomstick. She's maybe got this thing for appearing to be hysterical, you know? Like maybe she was locked away in a room with yellow wallpaper somewhere, but managed to escape through a window. Like maybe she rode a broomstick out of the asylum, right?

Here we are arriving at our next destination: Gander, Newfoundland and Labrador, a place of thirty thousand people with THE CROSSROADS OF THE WORLD as its tagline. It's right there on the sign by the highway as we come into the town, right beside the turnoff for the airport where, back in the 1940s, Gander was an important refuelling stop during the war.

And I'm wondering, as we zoom past that sign, if weapons and supplies were flown through Gander at the time of the rebellion in Spain—the-salt-of-the-earth Newfoundlanders helping Franco's cause.

Strip malls line the Trans Canada Highway. The dollar stores. A KFC. Tim Hortons with, like, a million pale and doughy, sandal-clad locals slurping and smoking and shuffling about. A gang of kids on dirt bikes blaze through the roadside ditch.

Look! A parking lot!

There are ungrammatical and possibly sarcastic posters advertising a rubber tire fire this very night. "PARTY!" "FREE!" "BURNING RUBBER!"

I look at Catherine, and she looks at me.

"Definitely," she says. "That is one *party* we shall not miss."

—— • ——

Everyone's shining their headlights at the blaze. And everyone is standing around the blaze, drinking. Someone has their stereo cranked: gangsta. The bass so loud you can hear the car's chassis rattle.

A pyramid of black tires, and black smoke retching up into the black sky.

Catherine disappeared twenty minutes ago with a group of young dudes: bro types with bad tattoos, gold chains. I watched her, surrounded, leaving the circle of firelight, and now here I am, waiting for her to return, imagining her off in a pocket of the gravel pit with a cock in each hole and a lineup of guys keeping hard and waiting their turn, urging on their homies (NO HOMO), while one of them works the video camera with a direct upload to the Internet.

I'm watching a toddler throw rocks in the fire. He's the last one left, that kid, most of the families have already gone by now. Covered in black soot while his parents are yelling about something or other, something "funny" that happened, and, through the smoke, way up high in the black sky, there's a plane passing silently above us, its lights blinking.

First time I thought about killing myself, I was fifteen. I thought: I WILL SHOW YOU ALL.

Roofies, rape culture, let's brutalize the fucking dumb sluts, cause they're fucking dumb sluts.

The little kid shouts: I'M BIG AND ALIVE!!! I'M BIG AND ALIVE!!!

My Sprite finished, I chuck the plastic cup into the fire.

It curls and shrivels and goes up, poof, a flake of skin.

And here's Catherine, dishevelled, black ash on her cheek, appearing out of the dark beside me.

"Joe-Joe, I'm too fucked up to drive."

I can't do it. I won't. My license expired while I was in Spain and no way will I get behind the wheel again. A flake of skin.

Her face has that look it sometimes gets when she's had too much. This sneering, pale mask.

"What," she says, "you're mad at me, now?"

One of the skeets drives us back. I'm in the back seat, listening to him and Catherine talk.

Likes: Kings Of Leon, Snoop, Gold, Weed, House, Tribal Tattoos, Ear Gauges, Dubstep, Cologne.

Dislikes: Fags, Girls Who Don't Shave.

Despite this, he actually seems like a nice kid. Doesn't drink.

"Why not?" Catherine asks as we pull into the parking lot of the Albatross Motor Inn. "Is it because alcohol reminds you of death?"

"What? No. I just don't like it, is all."

"Is it because drinking makes you think of killing yourself?"

"You're staying here, right?" he says. We're stopped outside the door and I've got my seatbelt undone, waiting for Catherine to finish up with the torture. I can see the night clerk looking out at us through the glass door.

"Maybe it reminds you of how fucking meaningless your life is," she says. "Or maybe it aggravates some intestinal problems you have."

I get out of the car, but because her window is down, I can still hear what Catherine's saying.

"Maybe you don't hate yourself enough, or maybe you're a fucking baby and they should lock you up in the mental. Maybe you're just a little rich boy who'll be running Daddy's company in a few years and you don't wanna fuck it up. Did he buy this car for you, honey? Or does he just buy the rohypnol?"

The kid leans across her and opens the passenger side door.

"Good night," he says.

I reach in and pull Catherine out of the car.

"Your wife's a cunt," he says.

"We're not together."

"Well, whatever," he says. "She is."

Catherine kicks the front fender.

"Thanks for the ride!" she yells as the kid peels off, the taillights gone down the highway just like that.

Then we're inside, past the night clerk with his celebrity magazine, and to our room where Catherine starts in, pacing the floor, to and fro, working herself into a frenzy: EVERYONE IN THE WORLD IS A FUCKING IDIOT.

Afterwards, I'm on the toilet, boxers on the floor, and suddenly, there you are, Lee. The mud-encrusted toes of your hip waders, the canvas-encased calves, the powerful thighs, the zipper that runs from your stomach to your heart. A red flannel shirt flecked with moss, bits of twig. Your bronze neck. My eyes fix on the bulge of your Adam's apple, the smell of woodsmoke, whisky, fresh water and wind. There you are, dear Lee, standing on the tiles of the bathroom of The Albatross Hotel.

"Hi Joe," you say.

Hi Joe. Not exactly the first words I'd expect to hear from you, but, nonetheless, there they are.

"Hi," I say.

"You're enjoying your trip?" The Adam's apple bobs.

"Yeah! Um, yes, I am. How are you?"

"I think you're meandering a fair bit, but it seems to be going okay as far as I can tell."

"Really?"

"It's passable, what you've got so far, but you'd better pick it up for the climax." You scuff the floor with the toe of your boot, as if to accentuate.

"I don't really know what you're doing here," I say.

"You're just a little lost," you say. My eyes come up to your thick neck again. "I like the turns of phrase you use. Some of it's quite beautiful, but don't get precious about it. Just do what you have to do. What feels right."

"Like right now?" I ask. Catherine has turned the TV on in the next room.

"Yep," you say. "Something like this breaks up how miserable you are. This lovesick thing that more or less seems to be the subplot, but you shouldn't be afraid of throwing us a curve occasionally. Just for the hell of it."

"Like I said, I don't know what you're doing here."

"I'm here because you need me to be, Joe. I'm here because you asked me to be."

"I don't want any of that magic realist stuff," I say. "I'm sick of that."

You shrug. Your hands come up. I see, surprisingly, how small they are. And the nails are clean.

"Call it what you want. You're the pilot on this trip, even if she's doing all the driving." You thumb toward the other room, where it sounds like Catherine's watching the ball game.

"I just want you to kind of hang around in the shadows," I say. "Like you're haunting the trip or something. It'll make more sense for what comes later. I don't mean to be rude to you, Lee, but, I mean, I address you constantly, and there are those scenes with you and Jack Samson talking coming up."

"About that," you cut in, "go easy with the homoeroticism okay? It's already in there. Don't be so obvious. You might want to cut that part. But, again, you're on the right track, I think. Keep going."

"Okay, okay," I say, realizing I've had the entire conversation with my pants around my ankles. "Just keep with the haunting though." I kinda hate how I sound right now. Like a kid or something. Totally Adjunct.

"Fair enough," you say, "but don't you think I should have some say in this? This is my name you're throwing around."

"I like it better when you just do as you're told."

"Well, that's never really been my cup of tea," you snort. "That's part of the reason why you're so enamoured of me."

"But what do you think of the whole letter-writing thing I'm doing? Like, does it just get tedious after a few pages, or what? You think it stands up to what Catherine writes?"

"Goodness, I don't know. I don't go in for fiction really. I'm more of a history guy. Science stuff. But I like what you have so far. Catherine's stuff I haven't read so I can't compare, and to be honest, even if I had read her writing, I wouldn't say anything to you about it."

"Why not?"

"That's between me and her, Joe. Mind your own business."

"Right," I say. "But this road trip. All that stuff. Seems good to you?"

"Yes, yes, enough already." You reach up and brush off some of the moss from your shirt. "Keep going. I'll talk to you later."

"Okay, fine," I sigh, and with that, dear Lee, you're gone.

"What are you? Reciting poetry in there?" Catherine mocks as I come out of the bathroom. It's the Seattle Mariners on the television. "I'm the one with the reading coming up, Joe-Joe."

—— • ——

DAY. THREE.

Gander to Grand Falls-Windsor

Al Pittman was once the most prominent poet in Newfoundland.

Legend has it he drank himself to death.

His kidneys and liver like blackened, withered fruit.

They say the morning he died his friends brought him in a wheelchair to a cliff overlooking the sea before dawn.

The great, grey ocean.

Seabirds, the smell of kelp.

The rising sun turning the wide sky blue and gold.

They'd tucked a bottle of whisky into the crook of his arm, and left him there looking out, knowing he had mere hours to go.

His notebook on his lap.

The sun a red line on the horizon.

And amongst that group of friends, they say, was Gerald Squires.

A painter and sculptor, Squires rose to prominence in the 1970s in Newfoundland for his landscape paintings, which were, more or less, allegories for life as the only people on earth to willfully give up their sovereignty.

I knew him. Soft spoken and mild and bearded with a kind of ferocious glimmer in his eyes—he died last year.

At his funeral I found myself weeping, Lee, though I didn't know him very well, just through the gallery—and people must have thought I was just faking it for my job or whatever it is that they thought I was doing—but anyway, I wept and was ashamed of myself and was thinking of Jess probably, like really, like deep down I was thinking of Jess and like the entire city of St. John's was there—my colleagues or whatever—everyone who had ever cared the slightest for art in Newfoundland—everyone crying—and they sang on the steps outside the Bascillica where the service was held, the *Ode to Newfoundland*.

About an hour's drive north of Gander, my lungs still full of soot from the bonfire, Catherine stops the car.

Beyond the gravel parking lot, and down over a curving wooden walkway, through trees whose leaves are heavy with water from an overnight rain, we've reached the interpretation centre.

I'm shivering.

"Ever heard of this place?" Catherine asks rhetorically, plucking a pamphlet from the little rack by the door to the building. It's a weird mishmash of teepee and longhouse, except with grey shingles and white vinyl siding.

She reads to me: "'The Beothuck—a unique and vibrant culture—now vanished.'"

I see our reflection in the glass door.

"'Vanished,'" she says. "Like a hurricane or something. Without agency."

It's too early, the door is locked, but Catherine leads me by the hand round the back. High, wet grass cold on our legs. I feel the Down Below bubble and stir.

A trail leads through the woods to a re-creation of a Beothuck village.

"'Imagine,'" Catherine begins reading again, "'a now extinct people with a unique language and culture.'"

She kicks a rock into one of the firepits.

The wind moves through the leaves of the trees.

Something's wrong.

I feel for the pill bottle in my pocket—that reassuring rattle—but they must be in the car.

"Come on," Catherine says, taking my hand again. We walk down the soft path that winds beside a river. In the distance, we hear a waterfall.

Along the trail, mushrooms gleam darkly amongst the moss in the shade of the trees.

Some small animal moves through the underbrush—we see the greenery move and hear the rustle.

Pine, tree sap, I smell the tobacco from Catherine's pouch as she stops to roll a cigarette.

Something is definitely wrong—my heart racing.

In a clearing surrounded by whispering trees, a bronze statue.

"Shawnadithit," Catherine says, but I already know that. There isn't anyone from Newfoundland unfamiliar with the story.

Animal skins and feathers in bronze. Her eyes—which are not eyes at all but rather black holes bored into the metal—look out behind Catherine and me into the middle distance.

This is Squires' most well-known work. I'd only seen images online before now.

A boat journey he took decades ago during which he claims to have seen her, or her ghost, or something, on the edge of some nearby cliff—staring out through rising mist at the setting sun. And so, years later, this is how she is memorialized. The last of her kind.

Freshly returned from U of T, I'd snickered at what I saw as Squires' racist pseudo-spirituality neatly coinciding with the demands of official memory.

And now, here I am, dear Lee, driving across this island, talking to you, a dead man.

I need to sit down.

"Fuck, Joe, you look like shit," Catherine says.

I kind of dry heave a couple times, gagging.

There are these awful retching sounds coming up straight from my diaphragm.

It's fast. Projectile style. I hear it land on the ground.

Acid in my throat. In my nose.

I kneel.

My eyes watering.

I see Catherine's face, and she's worried.

"I'm okay," I croak out, then puke a bit more.

Except I'm not okay, Lee—I'm going to die.

I look at the statue's face.

Catherine helps me to sit up.

I take a couple deep breaths.

"Wow," she says. "I've seen some serious criticism, but that takes the cake."

She smiles. I do too.

"Sorry," I say.

She wipes my mouth with the sleeve of her jean jacket.

I'm weak and trembling, and we go back to the car.

"Get some sleep," she says, starting the engine. "You scared the shit outta me back there."

Thump-thump-thump, dot-dash-dot.

I'm jolted awake.

There are bright eyes in the headlights, then nothing.

Car accident, see? Just like that.

"HOLY FUCKING SHIT," Catherine shouts.

I'm still groggy. Something dead in my mouth.

Car stops. Trunk pops. The interior light gushing out onto the roadside.

What the fuck is happening?

Catherine's out, her head in the trunk.

There: The Bible, The Thunderbolt, The Blessed Sprite all wrapped in a blanket.

"Flashlight," she says to the co-pilot. Me, the nurse, rummaging around, handing over a scalpel.

Code Red.

Mayday.

EMERGENCY.

We scan the ditches.

Juliette, Echo, Sierra, Sierra.

Juliette, Echo, Sierra, Sierra.

Yellow line, black road, white light in the sky—we hear it before we see it: black nails in a red paw on the gravel in the ditch. Something scratching at a door.

Who's there? Who's there?

You don't wanna know.

Catherine goes down in the dark to find the body.

Comes back up about a million years later with the thing in her arms.

I shine a light on the fox's crushed head.

"She's dead," she says, "she's dead."

The poor thing just bleeding like a motherfucker.

My heart still pounding and my head still dizzy.

Those sounds Catherine's making as she holds it—they're almost like the sounds she makes, late at night, her face right there above mine in the darkness. Her heavy breath smothering me. And I know, watching her there, that this is the sort of thing that gets right into your marrow.

Catherine saying, "I'm sorry I'm sorry I'm sorry," until the little thing takes its last breath.

—— • ——

The highway, the car, us moving westward.

Catherine driving with dried blood on her hands.

Her eyes red-rimmed.

We'd laid the fox's body on the gravel shoulder.

"What're we supposed to do?" Catherine had asked me.

I'd shrugged. Good question.

She'd gone over and put her hand on its neck one last time.

"Bye little buddy," she'd said. "I'm sorry."

And as we drive, for some reason—the fox, the Beothuck, Goodbye Goodbye—I'm thinking of our ten-year high school reunion. All those preppy boys and girls, now blimps, with weird lumpy bits beneath their clothes, nudging each other with their elbows as me, Martin and Catherine come into that old gymnasium, where the Heart boys basketball team (at which time was called, I kid you not, "the Hooters") had a home court record of 18–1 in 1992. The sole defeat coming when star point guard Timothy Whatever sat out with a broken nose.

Soft dim lights of pink and violet to flatter the suspiciously plastic-looking faces of what once was thought to be the most promising class of graduates the school had ever seen. Catherine's face so sweet and flushed, fresh from being picked up by her first literary agent, smiling away at all the old chums as though they'd never had a bad word to say to her.

Our school's most popular (and only) rock band, the Beautiful Losers, taking the stage. The sweat on the singer's head already gleaming. The light catching his glasses. Jowls swinging to and fro as the kick drum beats. Martin and I standing with our drinks while Catherine dances to one 90s hit after another.

Had it really only been ten years since the lawyer's son, the doctor's son, the son of the wealthy business man, had strutted those hallways, their chests and limbs hard as planks? The popped collars, the hand-me-down Beamer, the mushroom cuts. The ski trips to the Rockies, the cruises of the Caribbean, the weekend shopping excursions to who knows where?

Evidently, it had, and now, little bellies jiggled with abandon just above the waistbands of their relaxed fit Levi's. I later told Catherine how those wobbly bits reminded me of grilse totally going for the big leap over the falls. The bellies of my old schoolmates: a life and an animal intelligence of their very own, beneath the hot lights of the stage, in a last desperate spasm to recapture some teenage glory.

And then later, one of our old classmates asking, "So Catherine tell me—what is it that you do?"

"What do I *do*?" Catherine says. The vein in her neck pulses with a menacing rhythm.

The thrum of that fucking heartbeat in that fucking vein. I've watched it. Right in the middle of things, Catherine throwing her head back, just bam, like a horse tossing its mane, grinding away on me, that vein bulging out like a rope leading to heaven. Like a rope pulled taut from her heart straight through to her brain. A thread coming down to me, that pulsing artery, like a fishing line. And man, Lee, don't I take that bait every time? Don't I just love to see her like that, with her head tossed back, whispering in ecstasy, to quote a little Rim-bawd on you?

"I'm a servant," Catherine says.

"What?"

"Yeah. I'm a servant."

"Ho, ho, ho," says Martin, butting in. "She's writing. She's a writer."

"It's just a hobby," Catherine says, brutally. "I work in a restaurant."

"She's a server. Not a servant, ho ho." Martin's eye shooting around.

"Oh ha ha."

"She's just been picked up by an agent," I say, and Catherine, that vein pumping, giving me the death stare.

"Something wrong with being a server?" Catherine asks.

I recall, suddenly, the wonderful head-butt of years past, and grip my plastic wineglass full of Sprite out of fear or lust I know not which, dear Lee.

Catherine turns away, takes my and Martin's hands, and the three of us leave the gymnasium before even the Beautiful Losers have found their way off the stage.

POEM FIVE OF TEN FOR AND ABOUT CATHERINE PRINCE

When it goes right,
Isadora Duncan shits herself.

Apparently, that's what happens
when you die
of asphyxiation.
BOOM!

A load like a ten pound
cinder block. Except in this case,

it's a ten ounce tenderloin
you're about to pay fifty bucks for.

But anyway if Renoir were a waiter,
he'd love this shit.

The straight up poetry of it.
Because just then

your hands are also the hands
of the other servers,

and for an instant, it's not a shit job,
but a fucking symphony,

a ceremony, a ritual,
an epiphany.

It is
fucking experimental theatre,
but way better than that, thank God.
It is the history of the labour movement.
It is Ghandi, and MLK, and Spanish anarchism.

Your hands are the hands of peasants out of the foothills
and slums and shanty towns of Port-au-Prince.
Your hands are the hands of sex workers,
cab drivers, Walmart greeters
who are saying under their breath as you pass
Fuck You Fuck You Fuck You.

—— • ——

Don't.

That is, Do.

Not.

Piss me off.

I'll hold you up for the public mockery you've so long deserved (and much more sweetheart, see below).

Yes, rage. The sadness that fuels rage. Yes, doctor, yes. Both.

Six years, doctor, yes—that's how long it's been since the accident. After my first stint in the hospital, I "holidayed" in Spain.

I'll sit at my desk and suddenly realize the last two hours I've been staring at this list on my cubicle wall:

> Write essay on the beginnings of N L's tourism industry, circa 1942.
> Edit and revise by May 15th.
> Proofread by May 30th.
> Meeting with Peggy M BA, 1 PM, May 30th concerning above.
> To designers: June 1st.

But in reality I've thought about nothing but stabbing Peggy in the jugular using a pen emblazoned with the gallery's logo.

I'll picture Catherine sucking Martin's stump dick, and shudder, dear Lee—no joke.

"You cold?" Catherine asks beside me in the car. "Put your window up."

Martin, maybe, in leather chaps and all, dismounting a steed decked out in chrome and diamond skulls—riding a rainbow of sludge right across the sky.

"No more puking," Catherine says. "No more art."

The tip of that pen in my hand like the tip of a motherfucking warhead. Just wrap your fingers around that sucker: Ooh me likey!

Gasoline, gunpowder, fire.

Down the road me and Catherine skip in Martin's extravagant coffin on wheels.

List of things that had not yet happened in the little narrative that follows:

U of T.
MFA (Obviously).
BA (English). Not yet finished. (I / C) (?).
Martin.
Jess.
Nervous Breakdowns 1 and 2.
The turn of the millennium.
Lee Wulff obsession.
Pills (red, yellow and green).
Current Rage (Previous Rage was good to go).
Public demonstrations of outright LOVE blah blah blah blah.

This is me at the bar where Catherine worked back in 1995. And here she is, pushing ephedrine with the dark rum and cokes—a kind of chemical bipolar disorder—"Speed kills," she says to a patron "but it's also a hell of a good time."

A rundown little dive that, ironically, you climbed a flight of stairs to enter. (See: pearly gates, single engine planes, amphetamines (uppers), one's backbone (metaphorically, and its counterpart (by which I mean, literally: climbing stairs: that is to say, pain from one's ass up the black whip (spine, in this case unbroken, but in other cases (sorry Jess), severed as fuck), covered in bone (also unbroken, or not)—the severance of which renders language (secret or otherwise) unintelligible (this is the marriage of form and content)(again, sorry about this mess)).)

Pearly gates: Catherine's teeth. Man, what a set she has. That sweet mouth opening up for me (and, let's not tarry too long here, for many others), Saint Peter maybe somewhere back there in the dark as the jaws yawn, and her talking—flirting with some bearded biker dude—as Our Hero stumbles into that bar: those jaws working, laughing, to and fro, up and down—ha ha ha HA—whereupon I challenge the whole place to a fight.

Here's me, later: my arm draped around my pal, Rage, in some random pre-Facebook selfie. The whole place dead silent (severed spines and crushed skulls all around, maybe?) except for the music and Catherine's pearly gates just snap boom shut like an air compressed cabin door closing. No smoking, seats upright, and put that blind up mister, twenty total skeet dudes gone dumb from little Joe Penny, drunk as fuck and a spine made of what—fibreglass?—saying: I WILL KILL YOU ALL HA HA.

Five feet, ten inches, 150 pounds, brain like a bomb of bad wiring. A nest of red, yellow, and green. Catherine absolutely exploding (sorry everyone) cause here was her dear pal in a show of public something-or-other—saying "Joe, get the fuck out of my bar and I'll call you later."

Those teeth in their tender little pockets going up down, but I'll say this much about it: Not one of those woebegone love-struck tough-guy little dudes raised a hand or a peep—not even the biker, who only stroked his beard—and, shooed outside by the distraught Ms. Prince, dear Lee, dear Doc, you'd be so proud yet ashamed, when I smashed out the window of that second floor death trap with a piece of brick dug up with these very hands from some broken sidewalk right outside the door.

The voice of my heart—full of napalm and burnt bodies—going Fuck You Fuck You out on the street while my poor love slings drinks and amphetamines—whiz nibblies she calls them—until six in the morning, the meantime bringing wordplay for me in the mirror of my bathroom: me-anti-me, do you know what I mean by that?

> The morning:
> Rage right here on my shoulder, Catherine's drunken drugged up
>   voicemail messages saying:
> What The Fuck?
> Look Out For The Dead.
> Caution, Warning, Broken Glass.

Like I said, 1995.

It wasn't much later that Jess died on a curve of our beloved Trans Canada.

———— • ————

"Big money," Catherine explains as we pull up to the front of the building. The Dandelion, now in its twenty-seventh year, has become so bloated, the cultural demand so astonishing, that they've branched out to secondary and tertiary events; one of which is here, and the other somewhere up the Northern Peninsula, where the invited writers and the festival's attendees engage in something called "oral tradition."

What appears from the outside to be a rundown warehouse has been totally renovated inside—hardwood floors gleam and high-end antique furniture beckons as we enter.

Across the sturdy beams of the ceiling—rough rope and fishing twine spread in webs, and the walls bedecked in sealskin. A collection of hooked rugs showing the local landscape—green hills and white clouds and blue skies and birds in the air. In one corner, hip waders and bamboo fishing poles that look like they've never been wet. Above the mouth of the stone fireplace in the centre of the room, an unstrung fiddle and an accordion with several missing teeth hang from spikes in the brickwork.

We're early—no one's here but the host and his wife.

I'm struck by how young they look.

"John Wayne," he says in a Texas drawl, putting out a giant mitt to shake. He smells like maple syrup and the sea.

And as Catherine finishes introducing herself, he looks at me.

"You must be Martin," he says.

"Joe Penny," I say, while he crushes my hand in a death grip.

I look at my shoes.

"Charmed," says Isobel, the wife, who's unbelievably good-looking. In fact, I don't believe it. Those lips a shade too full. Her bust impossibly high and round.

After the cork on the champagne is popped—Catherine having told them I'm a curator—they lead us into an adjacent room —Isobel's studio.

On one wall, an enormous collage of celebrity faces—their identical smiles beside cut-out images of Big Macs and Coke bottles. Here, a hammer and crucifix next to Brad Pitt's blue eyes while a Whopper floats over his head like a halo.

"They're very impressive," I say.

Beauty products, cars, beach balls, kittens.

A yin-yang, a mandala.

Charlton Heston's head beside a pistol.

"I studied at RISD before going to Goldsmiths," Isobel says.

She's toying with the gold necklace that hangs in her cleavage, smiling at me.

"Mm-hmm," I say. "What kind of paste did you use?"

"Wheat." The four of us stand there uncomfortably.

"But." She raises a finger. "The work isn't complete without the performance aspect," she says.

Catherine shoots me a look, and as we're standing there, Isobel drags out two or three yoga mats from a closet and arranges them right there in front.

She ducks out of the room as John Wayne hits play on a tape deck.

Something ambient. With a didgeridoo.

Isobel comes back seconds later in a black leotard, her hair in a bun.

They put their heads together for a moment.

"You can do this, babe," I hear John whisper. "You got this."

They high-five.

She takes her place in the centre of the yoga mats.

A kind of pantomime occurs.

I can't stop looking at her feet.

I stand beside Catherine, fiddling with the cap from a Sprite bottle I'd taken from the car as the room fills with the slapping sounds of Isobel's footfalls on the mats.

After a very long time, around a minute or so—a crescendo in which Isobel has become a seed, a tree, a seed again—John Wayne hits stop on the deck. We applaud—slowly at first, and because the sound doesn't seem full enough—more loudly. Catherine and I exchanging looks with John's eyes on us. As Isobel, flushed and sweaty, hits the showers, he takes us out onto the back deck of the place to enjoy the sunset. Four Adirondack chairs and more champagne in a bucket wait for us.

And here—glittering in the slanted light—parked on the little gravel driveway that stretches behind the house below the deck—a 1980s Chevette spray-painted gold.

I can see along the windows of the car where whoever did it messed up the job.

"What's this?" Catherine asks, rolling a Drum.

John Wayne chuckles and shakes his head.

"Apologies," he says. "One of the local boys is something of an artist, too."

Isobel emerges from the house to join us.

Her drink refreshed, beads of water on her neck from the shower.

"I told our mechanic about that John Scott piece," she says. "*Trans Am Apocalypse*—you know the work?"

She fingers her necklace again, my eyes drawn to where her long neck meets her collarbone.

Of course I do. It's famous. The Book of Revelations scratched into the black paint job of a muscle car. I wrote about it for a paper in grad school.

"We let him keep it here while he works on it," Isobel says with a kind of half smile. "He calls it The Chariot."

I go down the steps of the deck for a closer look.

"What's scratched into the paint?" I ask.

Isobel and John kind of giggle.

"*The Dictionary of Newfoundland English*," she says. "But Bucky ran out of room only halfway through Volume One."

"Wow," I say. "Can I meet him?"

Silence.

"He's not available," Isobel says eventually, letting her necklace fall back between her breasts.

"He's gone to his cabin," John says. "Couldn't tell you for how long."

I run my fingers over where the letters are cut, and look up at our frowning hosts, and at Catherine, who flicks ash from her cigarette, squints down at me, and grins like the devil.

"*Paradise* seeks to address a people troubled by the secrets of their collective past."

This is Catherine's rather dubious introductory claim for her work. Her book reads to me like a standard coming-of-age-depravity-slumming-it-redemption-at-the-end story. But, the furrowed brows and milky eyes of the grandmothers here at John Wayne's tell me they're a) puzzling out what those secrets could possibly be, and b) they'd buy about anything Catherine would have to say anyway.

This sounds mean, but I'm being accurate. Social progress is measured by the comparative ignorance of older generations.

I'm sitting in the audience, smothering in the grandmothers' collective cloud of perfume, thinking about Bucky as Catherine reads—if I were writing a curatorial essay about it—outsiders, the working class, the oppressed—who seriously, would read it.

I like that he's done kind of a shitty job painting it. Technical virtuosity something I find so annoying. I think of how the bottom row of Catherine's teeth are just a little crooked—how I first noticed that about her one of the afternoons she took me to her trailer.

I know almost nothing about cars, but I do know that you can't kill a Chevette. Catherine's mom used to drive a red one way back when we first met. Over the years, as their trailer seemed to sink into the ground with entropy, that Chevette always ran true—the little engine turning over without a hitch even on the coldest days of winter.

—— • ——

Cathy, Martin calls her. That, or, sometimes *Cat*. Sometimes *Kitty*. Need I mention *Pussy*, dear Lee?

But for me, she'll always be Catherine. The Queen. Which is what she put on the cover of her novel: CATHERINE PRINCE. What I'd been calling her since Grade 10. Catherine. From the Greek, meaning *pure*.

Isn't that what you wanted, Lee? Purity? I wonder sometimes in your bush plane way back did you look down on that virgin wilderness and think of her name?

For in the darkness now of this ramshackle hotel, the silence out that window is so great that her name sounds in my head and in the beating of my blood, with a clap so loud you might mistake it for the roar of water hitting the bottom of the enormous falls on some undiscovered salmon river nearby.

Here on the bed, a note from Catherine, with a small stack of paper.

The note says:

I know this is the quickest way to end a friendship.

Will you look at this v. sad offering?

And under the note, this story:

> I'm a good boy I'm a good boy but I'm not a boy no more now I'm a man. That's what mom and jenny and dave said and that's what the policemen said when they said what they said about me on the video camera at the supermarket. Only I never did what they said, and I didn't do it the other time neither when they said what they said about me.

I'm a man now and I lives downstairs and jenny and dave lives upstairs because mom is with the angels and we buried her in her Guy Lafleur jersey only we didn't do that because they burned her up and put her in a genie bottle that lives in the closet upstairs in jenny and dave's bedroom. I'd like to rub that bottle and have mom come out of the top with three wishes for me because I know what I'd wish for only jenny and dave don't let me in their bedroom on account of how I went in there one time to see the genie bottle without permission.

And when jenny found me in there I was holding her bra in my hand that had been on the floor and I was just meaning to clean up and be helpful helpful like I was at the supermarket. But jenny said "Johnny, you are not to come into this room ever again without permission," and snapped the bra out of my hand and stuffed it into a drawer and pushed me back downstairs and slammed the door.

I used to work at that supermarket putting things in bags for people. But now I don't I don't. And the cashiers there called me Johnny Ditto Machine or Johnny Xerox because of my speech impediment that mom said was because I am a nervous wreck. jenny and dave would say it's cause I'm dumb but I'm not dumb I'm not. And at night I hear them fighting and it's got to do with how dave don't work and jenny says he's lazy and how did she get trapped into this thing? Then I hear them make up and they turn up the music which is always Honeymoon Suite cause that's jenny's favourite ever since she was twelve and she got their record with a heart-shaped bed on the album cover and spikes going through the bed like a bed of nails of nails for Christmas one year.

I'm a man now and that girl that girl I thought was my co-worker bending over stocking the toothpaste was not that girl but some other person who wasn't stocking the toothpaste but was a customer. And the police said I touched her bum and right there on the videotape they had it recorded and showed it to me and mom and jenny and dave but I didn't do it I didn't. Then they took me home and I had to return my smock and my name tag and a person from Services comes to talk to me twice a week about how mom died from diabetes last year and why I touched the customer's bum but I didn't.

And the man from Services is a man named Mark who drives a Hyundai piece of shit is what dave calls it. And me and Mark makes tea and play video games and talk talk talk talk talk for hours and sometimes not or we'll walk down to the stream and watch the trout at the bottom at the bottom because Mark says it calms me down calms me down watching the trout at the bottom at the bottom at the bottom.

If if I rubbed that genie bottle and mom came out I know what I'd wish for and that's to have mom's Guy Lafleur jersey back because when mom went to the angels Jenny packed all her stuff and a truck came and it went to the dump. We would watch the Habs game on Saturday night and mom would get all mad at Don Cherry and say things like "That man's a dummy," and that's how I know I'm not dumb because I'm not like Don Cherry and mom would be wearing her Guy Lafleur jersey and the Habs won the cup in 1986 when I was twelve and again in 1993 when I was nineteen years old and started working working at the supermarket putting things in bags for people and Guy Lafleur signed mom's jersey once at an old timer's game here at the Stadium.

But jenny said she wanted all of mom's crap out of the house and I watched from the window as the men came and loaded up and loaded up the truck. I imagined mom lying in her coffin at the funeral home wearing the Guy Lafleur jersey even though what really happened was the genie bottle on a table at the funeral home and Guy Lafleur won two Hart trophies and released a disco album in the seventies. And when I think about the men loading up the truck I feel like my head's gonna explode explode explode.

And I told Mark about the girl who I thought was my co-worker but was a customer. And that girl who was my co-worker her name is Jessica and one time at the staff party she pushed her boobs into my arm and pushed her lips into my lips and she sold flowers behind the counter at the supermarket.

And Mark takes me down to the stream after supper. When you throw bits of bread bits of bread into the water the trout come up to the surface. Me and Mark stand under the streetlight watching them. I can see their sweet little faces and their open mouths. The water is brown is brown and so so are the trout. Mark says I won't probably ever work at the supermarket again. I say that's okay that's okay but it's not okay okay because I liked working at the supermarket and Jessica's lips.

We're just standing on this bridge over the stream. Cars whoosh by on the highway. I try and think and try and think but can't remember the other wishes I had. When Mark drives away in his car, I always say "See you see you later later, Mark."

He puts up he puts up his hand and pulls out of the driveway and waves to me and we do it all again again the next day too.

I put the story and Catherine's note on the bedside table.

It's strange to think we've known each other so long.

I like the story. Catherine tries to hide how anxious she is about her second book, but based on what I've read, she needn't worry much.

I wonder what sort of trouble she's getting into right now, and arrange the pillows in the usual way.

Catherine, at my house one night, having seen this little bedtime ritual of mine had said, "You're just a little baby, aren't you?"

Her face changed. Her eyes were soft and she touched my arm.

"Sorry," she'd said.

After the reading and the questions that followed, I came back here and checked into our room. A motel with a Pizza Delight take-away counter in the lobby, where a slack-jawed redhead with a broken nose took my credit card number.

John Wayne fawning while Isobel broke out the whisky and I walked sadly here where the glow from the Pizza Delight sign cast down its golden light.

And in Spain the tiny rooms I was able to rent while wandering around were nothing more than cubicles. My office, my orifice, a jail cell, a coffin.

A sink in the corner and shutters that opened onto the streets below where the locals drank beer and watched the soccer match on television.

That's where The Motherfucking Bible started, Lee. Me weeping with a copy of *Bush Pilot Angler*, mining your text for words referring to flight, writing, the body, the senses. A room like this somewhere in Spain with me remembering how Jess and I had argued all day about what we were going to do. Were we going to go for it? I told her I didn't want to. I hadn't even written my book yet. She told me I was the most selfish person she'd ever met, and I said she was probably right on the mark. How was I supposed to write with that thing screaming and crying and squirting piss everywhere? I said: I can't even take care of myself, let alone someone else. She called the clinic right there. She wanted to hurt me. I went to the kitchen and poured up a nice one. The last whisky I ever had, because after she hung up, she packed up the car and out the door she went and I heard the engine start and watched the taillights recede from the window and I never saw her again after that, because it was only the next day I got the call from the hospital and that was that, you know, dear Lee?

Doc Sparling had said: Try writing it down. After you leave St. John's. What you're thinking about. It may help.

And so, here is Spain, and here is me, weeping, Lee.

To and fro, arrivals and departures.

When I wasn't underlining those magic words of yours—flight, writing, the body—*fly I write to see to hear to think*—here is me with a notebook trying to figure out what in the hell happened to me.

I thought I'd start with the morgue and the dude, the technician or coroner, having me see the body to confirm Jess's—whatever—but that didn't actually happen, so I didn't start there.

I thought I should just start with the funeral, but that didn't seem the best way to proceed, and then I thought I could start with how I met Jess in Toronto at a gallery opening and of how the light from a car passing outside the window lit up her face as she was being introduced to me.

Then I thought the thing to try was to start just before I met her, when I got my acceptance letter from U of T. But the more I thought about things the more they seemed to change in my memory so that, before too long, the bank account shrivelling and my arms hard in the farmland of Spain, I realized I'd failed Jess even in this. That I couldn't be true to her even in recalling the simplest things: how we met and fought and fucked and how she died, boo hoo, dear God, her body ripped to shreds.

I thought I'd try with coming back to Newfoundland, my bank account empty, and how Catherine picked me up at the airport. How she took me in Martin's car to the fast food joint drive-through window because I hadn't eaten anything, and how, in the parking lot, I begged, dear Lee, no joke, how I begged her to fuck me right there in the car, to take me back in time, you know?

I thought I'd describe how I intended to appear so desperate to her. And how, ultimately, I must have succeeded in this at least.

I wanted to describe how my love for Catherine sometimes, I suppose, reminded me of something the both of us hate: sentimentality in the service of forgetting the truth.

I tried by starting with Catherine, and as you can see, something about doing that has remained in the text because something about how Catherine was when we were kids and how she is now describes something about how I used to be and how I am now, and how that's a pretty fucking miserable thing.

But anyway, now (Who? Jess? Catherine?) stumbles in fresh from John Wayne's place, I can smell the whisky, the light from the sign outside making a halo behind her head, and she says, "Why, my little angel," and sitting on the bed, snakes her hand beneath the covers.

"I need you, honey," Catherine says later that night. Or morning. Or whatever. I've got my back to her, watching the window getting brighter as the sun begins to rise. Next to me in the bed, I feel her reach for the bottle on the nightstand, and hear the wine glug glug glugging into the glass.

"You know I haven't had it easy." She puts her fingers tenderly on my shoulder. Cold. Her hands always cold, even in summer, like the blood doesn't flow through there. She's always had poor circulation. When she's menstruating, she's prone to dizzy spells, dead faints just like that.

Once, in university, she just keeled over right in the middle of class and whacked her head on a chair before crumpling onto the floor. I was sitting next to her. Old Man Maloney, the prof, talking about Keats, didn't even notice. I saw how her pupils had dilated beneath her half-lidded eyes. They had this weird, shark-eye quality to them, reflecting no light. Someone, I don't remember who, called an ambulance.

"You don't talk about your childhood much," I say, the sun, now, here it comes. "You get annoyed with me for not talking about what happened, but you're the same."

"There's nothing much to talk about." I hear her sip from her glass. "But the point is, Joe, I'm grateful for you, you know? You've really given me a lot."

"I think about it like it happened to someone else," I say. "In a way, I can't even believe it was me. What happened before, know what I mean? I could just as easily have read it somewhere. Saw it on TV."

I feel her fingers warming up on my shoulder, like she's sucking the heat from my body.

"I know," she says. "And I know what a piece of shit I am—don't interrupt me. I know where I come from. I know, I know." She takes her hand from my shoulder, I can hear her voice tremble a bit. "I'm dirt, but at least I wrote a book." She refills the glass, it's Weepy Time. "People are impressed by me, I mean, look at me, Joe, I know what I look like. It's nice to be wanted. But you're the one who knows me best, honey. You're the one who's always been there. You know I'm trash, but you love me, don't you Joe?"

I've heard this siren song before, but it always works.

And I know, Lee, what you might have to say about it. I know I'm a sucker. I was born for this. That's why The Bible weighs on me like one of those big-ass radio cables they laid in the water by Heart's Content, which stretches right across the Atlantic to England. That's me down there, pinned to the bottom of the ocean by one of those things, bubbles out my mouth, because if I can finish this thing, this Bible, then won't Catherine just think I'm a swell guy. Won't she just drop everything and come running?

I'm about to say something like, I don't know, Lee: No I don't love you. Or maybe: Yes, I love you. But it doesn't matter, because, just then, her phone rings, and she's up, sorting through her clothes to answer Martin's call.

POEM SIX OF TEN FOR AND ABOUT CATHERINE PRINCE

CATHERINE ON CALL AT THE RESTAURANT, 1997

Fuckers. The moment you wake up
First thing you think is:
Do I have to work tonight?

Doesn't matter what.
Glorious summer day,
Girls in short skirts,
Cold beer and artichoke dip in the backyard,
The one thing on your mind
Is that potential call saying
You have to wait tables tonight.

And what's worse
Is sometimes the whole day goes by
And you're tied to that phone
But the call never comes.
Stuck pacing around the house or elsewhere
Dreading the pager vibrate
Or the land-line ring,
And meanwhile you could have gone
With me or Martin to the fucking circus if you wanted,
Smoked dope in the park,
Driven out to the ocean
Where the sound of the waves would say to you only that
You are free, free, free.

——— ● ———

We were S−C−U−M.

The Society for Creative Urges at Memorial.

That name is not a joke.

Also, we were scum.

Also not a joke.

An amorphous (not to say amorous) club of English major sideshow freaks ("I'm not an animal," Catherine would say in her best David Lynch *Elephant Man*) and a slew of others (law, chem, poly-sci, engineering) for whom something called Creative Urges seemed like a thing with which they'd be down or whatever, to remain grammatically correct for you.

GoD's little project through which he (amongst other things, as discussed: that is, Finger Banging) could separate the academic wheat from the chaff.

Urges: that meant acting or painting or something too, I guess, but who cared—not us writerly scum, or SCUM.

The real point was to try to tear new rectums for one another.

But the really real point was to put your work out there for criticism, only to ridicule those who had criticized.

I had this to say about, yes, *that* Martin's non-fiction piece about his WWI veteran great-grandfather's return, so many years later, to France:

IT IS A SAD AND REMARKABLE COMMENTARY ON THE STATE OF CANADIAN LETTERS THAT THE HORROR AND POIGNANCY OF WAR IN "NEWFOUNDLAND DEAD" IS OUTDONE BY A FOUR-MINUTE POP SONG BY BELLE & SEBASTIAN.

"Pfft," Catherine said, "this is hardly *Canadian Letters*, here, Joe, and anyway, saying something is remarkable and then going ahead and remarking on it is kind of redundant, don't you think?"

But this defence of Martin was just protocol. Your friends, or whomever in SCUM you may have been banging (finger or otherwise), could do no wrong in their writing, while everyone else was an idiot.

And it was here, in the dim and derelict conference room on the third floor of the Arts building where I encountered, for the first time, that tiresome species of literary bad boy, who, sadly, I've come to learn, is an all-too-common animal in the wilderness (tundra? That is, wasteland?) of the aforementioned CANADIAN LETTERS.

You know the ones I mean.

Portraits of Gide and Welsh tattooed on their ass cheeks, Bukowski's face on the head of their pricks (I don't know—when it gets hard, his mouth opens, or something, I guess (That is to say, dude's piss hole is Bukowski's mouth—saying something like: There's a bluebird in my heart but I'm too tough for him—or whatever—(Again, dear Lee, so sorry))).

Dive bar denizens, open mic maestros: laying out their frigging Dylan, Cash and Rolling Stones, and doing their best Mickey Rourke imitations—(*slurring*): A drink for all my friends!!!—a frigging ragged pocket notebook filled with scratches and a second-hand bookstore copy of, I don't know, Lee, *L'Étranger*—because, what they love is not being a writer (whatever that means)—it isn't the words and the sound of the words—it isn't the transformational, the communal—it isn't hope—what they love is merely the appearance of being a writer: the accoutrements, the sad little clichés—the booze and the sex and the rehab and the blah blah fucking blah.

"It's not the band I hate, it's the fans," said Catherine, bless her, after one of them (each unfortunate occurrence the Abu Ghraib of the SCUM meetings) would go through whatever "poem" or "performance piece" that seemed a rather prolonged mating ritual—like, *Look at me! Am I not the most hardcore motherfucker in the world?*

(Worst thing about it is: IT WORKS.)

All for the sake of banging some liberal arts first years—Freud? Fraud? Dear Doc, is it all just ego and libido?—because, let's face it, they'd prefer a cheerleader, but those chicks only go for jocks or cops or military dudes—hello, high school? You the same? Well, I'm not (LIE)—and Catherine at that time full on into her beloved postmodernists, had worked the word "cuneiform" into a poem about the rocks on Middle

Cove Beach—everything, dear Lee, even landscape—for her—a text—but thank GoD or God or whomever that that didn't last that long (ha ha).

SCUM: I met my first girlfriend who wasn't Catherine, and of course, Catherine hated her.

Lily (ironically: olive skin, dark hair, one beautiful Frida Kahlo unibrow (Sorry Catherine, Jess) (interests included: labour law, Howard Zinn, aboriginal rights): in SCUM she read poems about Reagan's Contra war, that is, how, like, totally totally shitty it was?—or whatever.

Old men/and oil/rule this world, she wrote, amongst whatever other sundry profundities, I can't recall, but anyway, the first time she read, I couldn't stop looking at her amazing, like, earth shattering tits (again everyone, so sorry).

When Lily and I arrived together at the second SCUM mixer—as we came in the door, I was describing, to her horror, how Jim Morrison believed the spirit of a dead Native chief had possessed his body as a boy—our future wunderkind, our Literary Star to-be, just basically ignored the two of us—except not—except withering glances, smirks et cetera—Catherine, so obviously pissed about it that Lily shortly thereafter just broke it off—"I don't know what's up with that, but the two of you have something to work through," she said, to her credit, and now, from what I've heard is—seriously, no joke—working in Geneva for the fucking United Nations.

Then there was Lucy the punk rock drummer, Lara, the art student, Lola, the ("artistic") dancer, Leigh, the activist, Leah, the (not so) secret lesbian—Catherine had said a list of those exes would sound like the first line from *Lolita* or whatever—and she'd said, further, they'd had all the combined gravitas of a used pillow sham—and had said, even further, that she knew it was serious with Jess because of that wonderful "J"—a hook, dear Lee—the only girl of mine Catherine could come to tolerate—"At least she's critical about things," et cetera—"And she looks good in heels"—or whatever—all of which really just meant she looked good but was not so good-looking as Catherine herself, which wasn't necessarily true—for the first time in my life, with Jess, I stopped watching pornography—and in this day and age (sorry), what more proof of love does one need than that?

POEM NUMBER SEVEN OF TEN FOR AND ABOUT CATHERINE PRINCE

B'ys, ah members now when ah was a youngster:
Fadder oot in de bowt in de wadder, jiggin' cawd.
An' 'e said to me wonce:
Nuddin' better den a fine day
to be at dat:
Jiggin' cawd.

By de fock—
Sun splittin' de rocks.
De fish, eatin' de rocks
(lots o' fish
In de wadder, ah means).

A dirty big grey 'ook
Come up
Oot de grey surf
Like de body uh Jesus
Goin' up to his own Fadder
In 'eaven.

Dat 'ook
Seductive now
As de words uh James Jice,
As me own aw-ten-tic vice,
As far as you
And dem dere cawd
bees concerned.

———— • ————

"GoD is a cunt!" Catherine says.

GoD: Gordon Devereux, the creative writing professor. He'd taken up reviewing books since retirement, and according to Catherine, wouldn't know a good piece of writing if it head-butted him.

This was when the very first review of *Paradise* came out in the local daily.

I'd gone to the pharmacist to pick up my prescription, bought the paper, and, having read the review while waiting in line, went straight to the liquor store to pick up the vodka for her.

Around eleven in the morning comes her signature pounding on my door.

Catherine on my step with the review crumpled in her hand, smudged mascara ringing her eyes.

I step aside and she stomps in, picking her freshly poured drink up off the kitchen counter.

"Thanks," she says, slamming it back in one go.

"It's just one review." I close the front door.

She paces to and fro across the linoleum.

"What do they want? What do they want?"

"It's just small-town bullshit," I say.

"What? Just cause I didn't suck his dick back in 1994? I don't believe it. It's class war, Joe. It's power."

She drops the ball of paper to the floor and stomps it one, two, three, four times, the glassware and plates rattling in their cupboards.

"And now what? Now I've gotta read from this piece of shit right across the country? A book tour—public flogging. Fucking torture."

I've heard her talk this way before—such contempt for her audience.

I take a step closer to comfort her, but she whirls around and looks at me, fresh tears making her mascara run down her cheeks.

"Those fucking cultural studies types. Those goddamn master's degree girls. I'm like a fucking case study for them. So like, what?" Catherine shatters her glass against the wall. "You're just the ones who considered me some kinda grotesque back in high school, right? 'Catherine Prince Sucks Cock In Hell,' you know? And now what? Now I'm your sexually-liberated working-class intellectual, am I? Now you're writing a paper on me, are you? Now you want to examine how I've articulated the process and means of my oppression? Gee, that's just swell. Thanks.

"And you know what's even worse than that? What's worse than having your life romanticized by a bunch of fucking vampires? It's that I've done it to myself. I'm the fucking vampire. If my mom were still around, she'd be so angry at me, I know it. I've turned all her misery into some kind of amusement. Just some kind of fucking intellectual game for rich people. For fucking rich people and their kids."

I grab another glass and I pour up another one for her. She swallows it.

She swoops down, and from amongst the shards retrieves GoD's review from the floor.

"GoD—he once told me I was a genius, Joe. Magic. And I was dumb enough to believe him. I took it hook, line and sinker."

She puts her head on the counter, bent at the waist like I've seen so many times before, only this time she's weeping, her shoulders shaking.

And I just wanted to say, like: What did you expect, Catherine? The entire book takes the piss out of Newfoundland and the publishing world, and then there's that bizarre scene at the end between the narrator and what heaven might be like or something, and the ending at the edge of that river.

Of course, I didn't say that, and even if I had, I know that the mention of the real G—O—D would have sent her on another jag, so why bother?

But it wasn't long before she forgot all about GoD's judgement, as it were, because soon enough, the national papers declared her a wunderkind, the new hope for Canadian literature, the next hot young thing, the rebel—and that first review looked petty and badly argued in retrospect.

But the eventual acceptance only led to more anxiety—the book deal, and the agent, and the PR and all the rest. For the first time since I'd known her, I saw Catherine petrified—a statue—in the face of expectation.

As for my opinion, I think Catherine's book is pretty good: beautiful in parts, and somewhat clichéd in parts, but not terrible. I guess you could say I like it well enough, Lee, but it doesn't really matter what I think, and anyway, like I said, we're back on the highway now and before too long we'll be in Corner Brook.

—— • ——

Sometimes I hear myself talk, and it's like Catherine's talking through me, you know? I can hear turns of phrase she may use come out of my mouth or whatever. See? Just like that. Sometimes I wonder if we mightn't actually be the same person, me and her. I'd like that, if it were possible. It would mean that I am, indeed, a wunderkind after all. And God knows I'm pretty enough to be a woman, though, dear Lee, I won't go on and on about it again like I'm prone to do sometimes, especially when I'm writing things down like this and the screen seems to have a bunch of holes in it, if you know what I mean. Letting all the flies in or keeping them out, depending on how you look at it.

For my graduate exhibition when finishing the MFA Curating, I brought in this artist originally from the Ukraine, who was then living in, like, butt-fuck nowhere Manitoba or something. Like, dude was living in a cabin in Churchill or something, I can't really remember. I think you'd like him, Lee, a real tough-guy artist type, which, like Catherine could tell you about writers, is just another type they pick up in a book somewhere and just go for it themselves, I guess.

Here's dude chopping wood, snaring rabbits, shooting moose or something, I don't know. Here he is drinking with the First Nations guys around the fire. Goddamn it, Lee, balls cut from stone, this guy, drinking the blood straight from the carcass of a reindeer, you know? Wearing its antlers on his head out in the freezing waste.

But anyway, I saw this video of his online somewhere and knew I just had to have it. That's the wonderful thing about curators, you know,

Lee, you only have to appear to do work. I mean, the job is just basically rationalizing why you pick the artists you do, but the work is already done for you pretty much, if you're capable of any kind of thought or what have you.

I think my dad would be pretty well pissed off if he were around, you know, Lee? His artist pals called curators the Freemasons of the art world, can you imagine. Like some secret cabal conspiring as to which artists are gonna get shown and the like, you know? At first, I thought this was pure illuminati crackpot stuff, but man, it sure doesn't take long to realize the truth of what Dad was on about, cause that's really it, you know? But then again, he was always suspicious of any kind of mechanisms of power, which he rightfully should be, I guess, and had therefore instilled that sort of thing in me. At least, he thought he had, though not well enough, apparently, because there I am every day, forming what he'd call Official Culture and Memory even though I'm just Adjunct and have hardly any power at all.

But back when I'd gotten accepted to school in Toronto, we had a fight about it. I think he was upset about my becoming part of the elite intelligentsia or whatever, you know? Can you imagine, Lee? Fighting with your parent because you're not undermining the dominant bourgeois society enough? You'd think I'd joined the Forces or something. Anyway, that's a story for another time, but just to go back to this video I was talking about for a minute, you should have seen it, it was really quite special.

It was just the simplest thing you could imagine. This Ukrainian guy, up in Manitoba somewhere, videotaped a moth one night at his screen door, you know? His camera had a light on top, and so all the moths and flies or whatever would just flock to his door when he had this light turned on, and he basically just films this one moth struggling to get closer to that light, right? And I remember thinking, that that was me and Catherine. She's the light, and I'm the moth, but also, it's the artist, right? Art is the light, and the artist is the moth. And I remember when we installed the video projection at the student gallery, how just like Pygmalion writing about Catherine would be. How, because she's the art, and I'm the moth (to turn things around on you), I was just bringing that sucker to life. And then The Bible and everything else that came after, dear Lee, why that was just a continuation of ripping off the idea behind this Ukrainian guy's video, you know?

Which, therefore, just complicates what I said above about Catherine speaking through me, you know, darling? Maybe what I'm saying is that by just writing about Catherine, creating her like I seem to be doing here in The Motherfucking Bible, I'm really just creating myself, you know? Or I hope I am.

But anyway, her hatred of creative writing teachers is based, of course, on those beautiful early days at Memorial University, when, upon receiving her Honours Degree, she tried getting into one of those programs.

The letters said shit like:

Unfortunately, we are unable to offer you a place in our program.

We think very highly of your work, but we've had a high number of exceptional submissions and are unable to accept you into our program.

We wish you good luck in your future endeavours.

You suck.

You may think you're doing something special and unique with your writing, but we've seen this a million times before.

You may be a star in Newfoundland, but this school is Big Time. And you aren't.

We know about the trailer you lived in, your French fries and Rice Krispies. You are not welcome here.

Using footnotes in your prose doesn't make it more enjoyable to read, and doesn't add anything to the text.

Signed, the Powers That Be.

So there you go. She hates those motherfuckers. And what do you think she did after all those rejections came back? Why, she just wrote her book anyway. The title derived from a town just outside St. John's where only now they've begun developing, where the subdivisions have begun to sprawl out as crass as one of those fake-titted ladies in your dad's porn magazines.

That's my girl.

And that's me there sometimes in the pages of *Paradise*: the ineffectual yet extremely handsome little man with a cock hard as marble. Get it? Pages 16, 20 and 36–45. Pages 110, and 116–131. Pages 300–303, and all of chapter 21.

Me, Joe Penny, like maybe I'm the statue brought to life.

And now, here's Catherine at all those dreary lit festivals with her top lip curled in a studied contempt for all those suckers with their tenured jobs. Knowing that the worst thing about it all is that her anger and hate have only made her one of Them, a CULTURAL GATEKEEPER, and no matter what, unlike me, Catherine Prince will always be trawsh.

Right down to the cold-tombstone-sharp-edged-eyetooth-shard of rock we call her heart.

POEM NUMBER EIGHT OF TEN FOR AND ABOUT
CATHERINE PRINCE

So anyway this goldfinch was on a branch
above my head, singing. I don't get many at my feeder
you know just the odd finch or chickadee but never a redpoll
and always the goddamn pigeons hang around at the bottom
waiting for some rare, random seed to fall
because they're too big for the feeder and it's designed in such a way
that it prevents them from getting their beaks to the food.

And so the goldfinch was tossing its head back and forth
because it was late April and finally the sun was shining
and God knows in his blue heaven I gave up poetry
because basically I suck at it
and its little voice was a picture of something else
like one of those pictures that's just a mess but
if you stare long enough
there are dolphins or periwinkles that come into focus for you
which is just a trick of letting your eyes un-focus a bit
ironically
and I thought
what the hell
might as well give it a try and see what happens.

So then I came inside and sat down at the laptop
and wrote this for you.
And so then therefore
I imagine the goldfinch on some strand of black wire
a telephone cable like a line of script
that for all I know might go right to the phone
God holds to his ear
on whatever bored afternoons I'm dumb enough
to even consider writing such lame-ass poems as this.

—— • ——

DAY. FOUR.

Grand Falls-Windsor to Corner Brook

Vroom vroom goes the car, and we go with it, the highway a black snake because they've put down new asphalt, and the west coast sun makes heat waves come up here, down deep in the valley, because the weather is so much better in Corner Brook than in St. John's and all those old mountains, bedecked in greenery and derelict ski lifts, surround us now and are pressing down upon our heads while somewhere up there in the blue, birds and bush planes whirl and are free and welcome us to the very beginning of the end of our journey, and furthermore, the story.

Up and down over hills we go, the black road winding and shimmering in haze at the horizon where the reach of our vision is met by the edge, and beyond, those mountains where your heart was shattered, where the Dandelion waits for us with its program of farce or tragedy I know not which, dear Lee.

I'm remembering Catherine at my apartment a couple years ago:

"So, I got Martin a present, but it's also for you, Joe-Joe," she'd said on the phone just five minutes before.

I know what that means. I unlock the front door. Clip my nose hair. Clip my ear hair. I turn on a few lights so she can see the place and not trip up over the stone pathway she helped me lay down last spring.

In she comes, in she comes.

Push-up bra and corset. Short skirt and fishnets. Boots, not cherry Docs like she used to wear, but something similar with this tartan pattern inside, and what gets me, of course, those laces undone, and the plastic ends click-clacking on the linoleum.

"What do you think?" She bends over the kitchen counter. That skirt, like a veil, ascends like a soul from some October funeral.

I'm thinking: Get me the fuck out of here, but not really. Really, I'm thinking, I want to have sex with Catherine. But also I'm thinking, how does one describe accurately their experience of beauty?

"Do you wanna fuck me, Joe?" she says. She's looking at me over her shoulder. She's fifteen years old, that's what she is. She's fifteen and I'm the age that I actually am. I get it, Lee. This is what it means to be a reactionary. If I want to fuck some facsimile of a fifteen-year-old then isn't that the same as wanting to reanimate the past? Even Franco, right now pulling levers in the Down Below, puffing his cigar, the ember at its tip throwing red light on the medals pinned to his heart—especially him—isn't he proud.

There's a stack of novels from the library on the counter which she pushes onto the floor.

I go stand behind her there and push into her with a hard-on that's about ready to burst right through my cotton slacks. "I hate these little prima donnas out there strutting around with their books," Catherine says to me over her shoulder. "They're obnoxious, Joe. They make me sick."

I've got a new pair of pants I'm trying, for the itch and burn, as it were. A little flower blossoms right where the head of my cock is fighting through the blue fabric. "Christ," says Catherine, "they'll try to take some other writer apart in a review or in their own book and meanwhile they're jumping through the same hoops just as much as whomever they're trying to take out, you know?" She looks back at me with this pained look. "It's as bad as actors. Like, 'Look at me, look at me!' all the goddamn time, baby. It sickens me." A flower a little darker than the colour of these pants, and I'm wondering seriously, in the midst of this experience of beauty, how come I feel so sad and exhilarated at once?

"You must see it pretty often at the gallery, huh, Joe? Your little art-school girls." She hooks her thumbs into the waistband of her underwear, and pulls them down slowly, pushing backward into me. She may be pushing forty, but her ass could still destroy the universe.

"Everyone trying to outdo each other all the time, I mean, how tedious can you get?" She braces her hands on the kitchen counter. I grind my pelvis into her. "Not that I know what the alternative may be. And to be honest, mostly writers are just the dullest motherfuckers in the world, and I guess that's due in part to them being show-offs, you know?" She flips her hair, looks back at me again. Catherine so full of bombast—a cover for her insecurities, literary and otherwise—complaining about show-offs. I undo my belt and let my pants drop to the floor.

I'm wondering if that isn't what really everything is all about, you know? This contradictory feeling of being miserable and just so, so alive and sad and wishing you were dead. Cause that's what's happening right now.

It's the night before I'm to take Martin to Metcalf's Falls—where my dad first taught me to salmon fish. It was Catherine's idea. Her saying it might be good for him and I to spend some time together—her lover and her best friend tramping through the woods to the river where I watched my dad's hands build fire for the first time. Maybe Martin and I would actually become friends.

He picked me up in the Crown Royal that morning in darkness. The city absolutely silent. And silent the car on the grey road.

The sky lightening now on the highway as we pick up coffee at the gas station along the way. I watch him pour four packets of sugar into his cup.

There's a place off the road where I get him to pull over. A piece of orange surveyor tape marks the trail that leads to the river, but it isn't really a trail at all—no one comes in here anymore.

Here's a photo of me on the banks of the river in 1980. I'm six years old and holding up a salmon that Dad had caught—its silver body awash in blood that runs from its gills, where I'm holding it—two fingers plunged into the gap below its head. I'm smiling, blood running down my forearm.

You know the world isn't such a sweet place when you've watched your father club a salmon's head repeatedly off a boulder, and that's what I'd done, just before the photo was snapped.

Martin is so artless and slow, I leave him behind in no time, but I stay within eyeshot—leaping over rocks and enormous puddles of mud and still water where flies dart up. Dragonflies hovering in the air. A grey jay trembles on a branch. I perch on a rock and wait for Martin to catch up—red-faced, the legs of his jeans dark blue from the water and mud that've come up over his waders.

"I fell down back there," he says. "This is tough going."

He leans on a nearby tree stump.

I'm wearing old hiking boots with supermarket bags for lining, but my feet are soaked. At that point in my life, I'd never spent much on gear.

Without warning, I throw him an apple from my backpack. It tips off his fingers and lands in the mud.

"Probably another two hours or so," I lie, looking at the red fruit.

He crouches to pick it up, knee bones cracking.

He holds the apple by the stem, and hesitates.

"Mud won't kill you," I say.

He wipes the mud off with his sleeve and studies the apple.

A worm seems to move in his brain, and he looks at me.

"I'm glad we're doing this," he says.

"You ready?" I shoulder my backpack and start off without waiting for him to answer.

A little while later, I'm waiting for him again.

It's an enormous bog we're crossing. Buzz of mosquitoes, and that humid marsh air pressing down. He's way back there, and my eyes are drawn to the distance—the same wooden fence with the same illegible sign nailed to it that I see every time I come here—but I'd catch it out of the corner of my eye while walking and always mistake it for a caribou.

When Martin finally catches up—I'm wondering what I'd do if he had a coronary—the red ball of his heart seizing up—I tell him about the fence and the trick it plays on my eyes.

He laughs.

"Like a caribou's just standing there forever?" he says.

There's sweat dripping down his brow.

I give him some time.

He chugs water, then soaks a rag and wipes his face and neck.

The mosquitoes are at the buffet, a swirling nimbus of them above his head. And on his face, already several doozies.

"When we make camp, you'd better put calamine on that shit," I say. "You'll crack up. Bleed to death."

"I don't have any," he says.

"Oh." I look back over to the fence in the distance.

"How much longer?"

I don't answer, but turn away and start walking again.

Without saying why, I tell Martin to busy himself snapping big green boughs from the evergreen trees, while I cut the right sized logs with the hatchet I brought. I weaken a log first with a couple of chops. Lean it against a rock, and stomp it. There's a nice, satisfying cracking sound as my weight comes down. I look at the back of Martin's neck as he's turned collecting boughs.

I like having him working away without really knowing the purpose of his efforts, but it becomes clearer to him once I've erected the lean-to. I'm not thrilled with sleeping next to the guy, but I'm not about to build a second one just for him, and I have him lay the boughs he's collected on the ground inside the lean-to for our bedding, and then atop the exterior structure for the roof.

Now, it's the river. I wade out to the big rock where the river rushes into the pond. I'm up to my waist and shivering already, my feet slipping on the rocks below the surface. A false step and the treacherous current will bring you under—B A M—like that.

The salmon always lie right here, resting before moving up toward the falls against the current. I climb onto the rock and scan the dark water at my feet. There's a deep pool of calm water that the rock creates in the current, but I don't see anything down there.

It's this weird trick you play with your vision—evolution has made salmon backs the exact shade of the river bottom—so you kinda have to squint your eyes and un-focus them at the same time to see them.

There's nothing—it's early in the year and besides, the water level's low. The weather's been too sunny.

I look over at Martin on the riverbank. The calamine lotion I gave him making his face a mask with these hideous red bloody streaks from the bites. He waves. I turn back to the river and cast, the fly coming down soft as a kiss on the surface.

There's nothing—not a fish to be seen in the whole river, and I wade across and back up to the campsite as the sun sets.

He's managed a fire, pouring a flask of rye into a tin cup.

"Guess you didn't catch anything either," he says.

"I'm catch and release anyway," I say.

That's pretty much all the talking until late into the night. He's drunk, and maybe on something, I don't know. We're sitting by the fire and he's muttering to himself. Shaking his head. The jaws of the grub begin to work again.

"My dad was bipolar. I ever tell you that?" he says.

"Nope."

"Yeah, no, he was though. It was hard as a kid."

The calamine and blood have dried into this crusty paste. He looks like he's been out here a couple weeks.

"It'd come out of nowhere," he says. "Like, it was really unsettling. Just up and down, you know? Constant."

He scratches his head kind of furiously.

"Anyway, sorry—it's none of my business," he says.

"Yeah," I say.

"At his funeral, people said he was at peace now. I hate when people say shit like that to me. Nobody knows anything for sure." He gestures in this sweeping way, spilling his drink.

"I gotta piss," I say, getting up and walking out of the firelight.

There's a big beautiful moon shining down. I hear the trees creaking in the slight wind that's picked up. Otherwise, it's just blackness.

When I get back to the fire, Martin's asleep. I look down at his face. I stand there like that for a few moments, and then I put my hand on his shoulder to wake him.

There's a moment when our eyes meet. I look at the fire.

Beside me in the lean-to, he snores the night away, but even if he didn't, I wouldn't sleep. I hardly ever do when camping.

On the way out a couple days later, we pass the bones of an actual, real-life caribou.

"Guess your imaginary friend didn't make it," Martin says.

We walk out to the road where the car waits for us.

And look, Lee, maybe I haven't been totally honest with you throughout this little thing I'm writing, you know? I've needed to change a few things for the sake of the book, I guess, but anyway, it's a totally different story, a totally different book, maybe one I'll write someday after Pedlar publishes this one, but there's a girl out there who may or may not be reading this right now (and I don't really suppose she is) for whom some of these scenes will be very familiar, and it doesn't make any sense in terms of this narrative to even be talking about it, but Hey, you, girl that I hung out with that summer, I just want to say Thanks or whatever. I know you couldn't care less, and you hate me now, but I just wanted to say that, okay? You really helped me and I won't forget you, all right?

That said, Lee, we can continue with the main narrative at hand.

POEM NINE OF TEN FOR AND ABOUT CATHERINE PRINCE

THE THUNDERBOLT!

Black. Coal black, and shiny. Seven feet and light as anything. You can't even feel that sucker when you've got it strapped to your backpack. Artisan fly rod, handcrafted in Lexington, Virginia, and sent to me during the winter, the very dark winter, as I gazed at that river on my screensaver at work.

Obsidian javelin. If Zeus threw lightning bolts, then call me Zeus while I've got this piece of genius in my hands. Exclamation point, phallus, big black dick. He's still a virgin, but not for long. Not when I get to the river, dear Lee, and dip him into the wet.

Magic wand, conductor's baton, light-sabre.

Yoda's voice: Splinter of night sky, this is. Catch salmon, many you will.

My THUNDERBOLT hums like a motherfucker when it cuts the air. Like the note from a Tibetan Singing Bowl. Just meditate on that for a sec, little salmon, I'll say, perched on a rock by the river watching the past go further and further away on the current. Om!

A quill. Ink as black as your pupil with which this teacher, your Jedi Master, will write across the sky: THE THUNDERBOLT WUZ HERE!

Six hundred bucks, and think that bothers me? When it arrived in the mail and I opened that box, I worried my face might melt from the power and the glory, if you know what I mean. Ka-boom, my THUNDERBOLT, the shape of a death-ray shot down from some satellite out there in the blackness of space from which this bitch was forged.

The THUNDERBOLT is the embodiment of the mystery of light crossing the universe as both particle and wave.

The THUNDERBOLT Dark Matter.

A rapier.

No, Excalibur.

A freak occurrence of nature.

One of the Six Strings That Drew Blood.

A note. Saying: Watch Out!

A semiquaver.

It's right here in the trunk of the car, as menacing as an M–16, right beside The Motherfucking Bible, which sits in a box wrapped in a blanket like my very own IED.

KA-BOOM! I say.

The sound of a bush plane's gas tank exploding.

Hear that, suckers? Hear it, world?

That's me, baby.

That.

Is.

Me.

—— • ——

"The only hope for the world is people reading novels. Or buying them, anyway."

"Huh?" This seems to come out of nowhere.

"I'm talking about empathy," she says. "You know? Feeling something for other people. That's why people like us are saving the world, Joe. You and me." We're driving nearer the west coast of the island. We see the mountains in the distance and this curious, purple mist around them. "I mean, this is why women are superior to men. The research bears this out, honey. Seventy-five percent are female. The ones that read novels, Joe. You can guess what the implications are."

"No." I say, "What are the implications?"

"You ever feel love for somebody? Sometimes I meet people and there's so much love for them that it almost feels like I'm gonna puke my heart right up outta my throat, you know, Joe-Joe?

"It feels like I'm gonna puke my heart up and then my heart will go over to whatever person it is and shake hands with that person, know what I mean? I'm saying, like, literally. Like my heart with all its gore and ventricles and whatever else will come out of my mouth and shake hands with the other person. That's what it was like travelling around, reading," she says.

The ditches at the sides of the road look impossibly deep. The sun going down, and in the bottom of those ditches filled with still water and litter there's another type of life happening. Mosquitoes, flies and frogs maybe down there in the murk feeding on something and fucking getting on with it. Whatever it is. That's culture. Culture is a layer of pond scum left to multiply. It's a fecund environment filled to the brim with filth. I think of my job at the Gallery and of how, every day, someone the night before wipes everything down with a mixture of vinegar and water. The urinals smell of piss and Comet. I've got pounds and stacks and stacks and pounds of files sitting somewhere with the names of every artist I've ever met scrawled on them. Letters saying: Pick Me. Please Like Me. All I want is a single letter saying: Fuck You. I'm Pond Scum.

"The implications are," she taps cigarette ash out the driver side window, "that women are more pre-disposed to feeling empathy for other people. Women, unlike men, are curious as to how it might feel to taste what another person tastes. To know what it feels like to be another person coming, you know, Joe-Joe?"

"Yeah, well, that's only because of the disposable income and free time," I say.

She's taking us to the opening reception at the house of one of the university profs, one of those enormous homes done in the style of the Old Timey Newfoundland fishing warehouses. Rustic, yet elegant. Clapboard. A simple, bare rectangular shape. Big windows. Back in the day, this style of structure was where the fisherman stored their nets et cetera, but in recent times has been reclaimed by our betters to express how in touch with our history they are. Think early 20th century utility reimagined as well-to-do simple living.

The driveway is full, and the quiet road, sheltered by oak trees, is lined with cars.

We park a ways down, and getting out of the car, I watch Catherine do a couple bumps off the point of a key.

"Sorry," she says. "This'll make me more anxious, but I need to be up."

She brushes her nose a few times, smiles at me.

"It's okay, Joe," she says. "Hopefully this won't take too long."

We walk up to the big house, there's music, the big windows are bright with yellow light, people's voices, laughter.

We come into the crowded living room.

Someone says, "Catherine and Martin are here!"

And—the coke kicking in—Catherine talking non-stop—like, a billion visits to the washroom—while myself and the rest of the congregated mass are stuttering and mumbling our way through introductions and small talk, everyone (but me, of course, Lee) just slamming back their champagne, whisky, vodka, beer, whatever. Our host (the elderly professor of English, I think) negotiating his way through forgotten names—"And how do we know you?"—the "we" I guess meaning the cultural and intellectual elite, such as it is blah blah ("No, my name's Joe Penny.")—(the Down Below in full revolt, dear Lee, Franco stubbing his cigar on the red wall of my intestines)—only to be rejoined, momentarily, by our Literary Star, that mouth going: "And then, and then, and then...," those teeth, that tongue, as mentioned, Lee, in constant, fluid motion.

An eternity later, I finally catch her in the hallway as she's coming out of the bathroom again. This time yammering to some new friend of hers (sweater vest, striped tie, bad teeth, dishevelled) and I say to her I've gotta get outta this place. I watch the muscles of her face just working away, the molars grinding against each other, she's like, "We've been here an hour, Joe, but yeah, cool or whatever, let's split."

As we're about to do so, we hear the ding-ding-ding of a knife tapped on glassware in the living room. Our host on a chair with his wine glass in his hand. A semicircle of his guests around him, looking up, and standing beside his chair, a bearded fiddle player plucks a few strings to further quiet the crowd.

"I just want to welcome everyone to the Dandelion," he says, three happy notes sound out from the fiddle. "We've had people visit us here for this event from the four corners of the globe, from all walks of life, some of whom are here tonight." He looks out into the crowd. His gaze lingering on Catherine beside me. "Al Pittman loved get-togethers like this. He loved music, good times and laughter. He loved art and he loved literature." A smattering of polite applause from the guests. "We miss him a great deal here at the Dandelion." A sombre melody from the fiddle. "He would have loved to have been here with us all this evening—it's almost like—well b'y, it's like he's here with us right now." More applause. I see some young guy, his cheeks an astonishing shade of purple, wipe his nose with a tissue. "But Al also loved dandelions themselves—in tea, and in cooking, yes, but also in what they represented to him—survival, determination, strength, stubbornness—qualities required of an artist." The sound from the fiddle builds in volume—there's tension hanging in the air, the melody becoming slightly more hopeful. "I better stop," says our host, wiping his eye. "I'm liable to tear up here and embarrass meself." A few chuckles. The room is sweltering. I feel Catherine fidget beside me. She grips my hand till I think she might break it. "Anyway, if he were here he'd want to say you're welcome. Enjoy yourselves, and enjoy your time at the Dandelion." The fiddle begins softly the first few phrases of a traditional reel, the host raising his hands over his head in supplication or prayer or communion, his eyes squeezed shut. "Welcome, welcome, welcome!" he shouts as the bearded musician bursts into his tune, the host climbing down from his chair as the whole room breaks into hand-clapping in time with the fiddle.

Catherine pulls me away, shaking her head.

But the worst isn't over yet, because the worst thing is that as we're cutting through the kitchen—an accordion and tin whistle breaking out behind us—"Fuck, we're surrounded." I say—I see that everyone has begun to eat from one of the huge stew pots that are bubbling on the stove.

"Smells like rabbit stew." Catherine wiggles her nose.

I'm watching everyone pouring it up into bowls and eating it, the air thick. The musicians playing more and more furiously. An old woman sucks a bone, while a teenage boy does likewise. And for one horrifying moment, it seems everyone is eating not the rabbit stew, but something else—"We've got to get out of here," Catherine says, her eyes wide.

We push through the crowd to the door, the air cool on our faces as soon as we get outside.

"That will never get old," I laugh, as we tramp around through the garden and finally out front. "He does the exact same speech every year, I've heard. The same eye-wipe. But the fiddle is a new touch."

Down the way to the Crown Royal we go, and finally to the hotel where our rooms are waiting for us—separate, of course, since Martin's here late tomorrow night—and Catherine, who's been chewing her lip, takes me out to the little balcony connected to her room and smokes, smokes, smokes her hand-rolled cigarettes.

"I don't know, Joe," she says, flicking ash. "It may be an act now, but once it was real."

"Yeah, but Al died twenty years ago."

"What's that remind you of?"

"Anyway, I still can't believe the crocodile tears," I say.

Catherine just looks at me. She throws her cigarette over the rail. We watch the red ember twirl to where it disappears into the darkness.

Catherine's hands trembling because she's so coked up, but also because social gatherings like that one make her nervous—puking, more often than not, in dozens and dozens of bathrooms from here to Istanbul. In the alley outside the venue where she's to read, or even once, she's telling me, into her purse before taking the stage. It's not everyone's eyes on her that causes the trouble, she doesn't really know what it is, the play-acting, the small talk, the ceremony of it all, maybe, the suspicion it's all bullshit and she just wants to go home or be alone or whatever—that she's trawsh, and that, here she is, performing her little role for everyone again—when the thing that makes her happy is not the tiresome elaborate pose that goes along with the readings and book signings, but just the words themselves, you know, Joe? The way they look and sound together on the page or when spoken aloud and yes, what they mean and where they come from, how those words really are alive—but really how when she's really on a roll and it's just her and her laptop in her third floor studio in Martin's enormous house, how the words are a hatchet chop to that old way of seeing things, and this new thing—as sudden as a car accident—kaboom, like that—this new thing, a vision, makes her feel less alone in the world (even if nothing at all really changes, it seems like it has)—is something, somehow, she feels she can share so that, who knows—maybe we'll all feel a little less miserable, maybe the world will change, maybe there's still some magic left—because even if we all will die, she says, for my benefit, I think—there's still something that's worth looking for, you know?

DAY. FIVE.

The Dandelion

POEM TEN OF TEN FOR AND ABOUT CATHERINE PRINCE

Sometimes I'll picture Martin
Pulling up in that silver Crown Royal
Right outside my house.

Me drinking a Sprite, editing,
Or otherwise practicing my cast
On the little front lawn,
And, seeing him there,
Will think,
That's right Troll,
BRING IT
Or whatever.

Him slamming the car door and coming up the steps
To kick my ass
Because I had Catherine wear those thigh-highs that night,
Because he hadn't bothered to bang the poor girl
For months and months on end,
Because I titty fucked her right here on this bed.
Or the truth,
Which is that he's as boring as fuck.

And anyway,
Her and I pre-date that little fucker,

But up he comes
And Dad, Lee, all of you,
Hemingway, Cervantes and Galway Kinnell,
Iggy, Chuck Berry and the rest,
You'd all be so proud

When I plant that can of soda,
Like an orchid, or tulip or something,
Square
Smack dab in his forehead,
Right between his good eye
And the other.

Or, even better,
Pluck the bad one straight out of its socket
With a cast so pure,
A line and lay
So fucking perfect,
That the hook goes in
And pulls the thing out
Without a sound.

Without even the tug
You might feel
Under other, less perfect circumstances
On the river,
Where some thirty pounder
Comes up for the fly
Out of the rush
Where the current breaks
Over the rocks.

And the red muck
Attached to Martin's eye
Is some bright
Holiday streamer
Arcing through the brilliant air.

— • —

Appear to be cool.

Don't try too hard.

Be nonchalant.

Yet, be passionate.

Be professional, yet seem rebellious and dangerous.

Read more.

Be less critical.

Become less political.

Be cool.

Just, be, cool.

The literary agent says, "You've written probably the best line in the history of English literature: . . . *until the tissue collapses under its own weight and you're left with a skull, filled like a bowl, to the brim, with porridge, that used to be your ability to think.*"

She laughs, and her laughter is not laughter, but is rather a three-tone chime on the door that announces how I've arrived, you know, Lee?—like, I HAVE ARRIVED.

Her face still flushed, the bedsheets strewn, and out the hotel window, Manhattan gleams in the sunlight. Later today, the bigshot meeting with Paramount—when in through the window a hummingbird flies to perch on my outstretched hand.

That's what I was gonna write about the agent, you know, Lee? In another one of those fantasy sequences that snaps back to reality.

I had something else planned with some dinner party, and, like famous people or whatever all telling me what a genius I am, but what's the point?

The way it actually goes is that I'm lying in bed watching sports highlights—I hate professional sports—Dad saying to me as a kid how it's just one more method of control: tribalism, irrational devotion and violence. I'm thinking about what I'll say to the agent to impress her.

Except it's not really impressing her that's at the heart of it. I'd settle for not appearing stupid.

The world is ending—and what do you want? To fictionalize your life and have young women suck your dick for it.

Murder and rape on a mass scale.

Your girlfriend dies with your unborn baby in a car accident.

You suspect that life is terribly meaningless, and you also suspect you're not even really an artist.

You're nearly forty years old and you're just as fucked up and confused as when you were a teenager.

The replay shows some monster dude crushing a fastball into the bleachers.

He's like Stephen King or something (except not, because that's much too crawss—dude's more Ken Goldsmith), and I am who I actually am—not in the dugout, or the minors, or even the stadium—just some wannabe watching the highlights.

The literary agent is trim and chic with straight cut bangs and a bob that's totally, like, dominatrix. Black and thick, her hair like a wig—film-noir-femme-fatale-best-not-fuck-with-me style—she says:

"You want to be a what?"

"A wunderkind," I say.

"A wunderkind."

"Yes," I say. Crossing my legs helps.

"You okay?" she says.

"Yes. It's these pants." I pluck the fabric of my wool trousers between my index-finger and thumb. "Itchy, you see," I say.

I put The Bible on the table between us. Such a small stack of paper. Such an incomprehensible waste. If you say the words of a dead person the right way, in the right order, like an incantation, can you bring them back?

"Right," she says. "So what's it about?"

"Well, my doctor says it's what comes from sitting too long. My place of work requires me to sit for long periods of time, and apparently that's a cause. But it could be other things. Anxiety, for instance. I don't think I worry much about things, mind you, I mean, my job pays well enough. I'm a curator."

We look at each other.

"I'm talking about your book," she says.

"I'm sorry." I put my hand on The Bible. Something about doing that makes me even more nervous. I notice, over her shoulder, behind the bar, a photo of Al Pittman with a pint of Guinness at his elbow. I can't stop looking at it.

"Ms. Prince says you've written a wallop of a novel. Part *Don Quixote*, part *On the Road*."

"She said that? That's nice of her." I don't say that Catherine's never read it. And I don't say The Bible isn't really a novel. I don't say anything more for a moment—reverting back to the awkward robot professionalism of the gallery.

See, I have a problem. Often enough, when the yokels come into my office with their slides, I detect that the given artist is a little nervous and weird about talking to me. See, they've got so much riding on this thing, and they don't want to mess it up. So after the tech has dug the slide projector out from whatever crypt we've been keeping it in, and we've gone through the paintings of cod traps, sunsets, seagulls, dudes done up in slickers, laundry on a line et cetera, there's always time to get the soup du jour, the salty dog, the humble Newf Van Gogh to kind of choke out a few words or what have you about how meaningful their practice is, cause, I don't know, Lee, pick something out of a hat, their grandmother had Alzheimer's, their kid brother committed suicide, their wife died of cancer, the sky is blue, whereupon, I confess, I kind of needle them with a bit of the ol' MFA Curating degree, you know? I kind of pester them with questions about class, or feminism (if they're a cunt), or Guy Debord or whatever other name I can drop, just to see what way they writhe, you know?

And so here we are. It's me and Trina. At least, that's what I think her name is. No. I know it's not Trina. It's something else. It's like ethnic, or something. She looks kinda Greek or something, but I can't remember the name.

I realize there's been a too-long period of silence between us.

"It's beautiful," I say.

"So it's about beauty." Not a question, there, Lee, and I realize it's probably the last thing I should have said about it. About The Bible, that is.

"It turns the coming-of-age story inside out," I say, a direct hatchet job from a quote I read about Catherine's book, and something that really has nothing to do with The Bible at all.

"I see," she says. She flips her little appointment book closed, looks over my shoulder at the waiter who's just gone by, and suddenly it dawns on me it doesn't really matter much what I say. I already understand too well my little outport Impressionists. I already get I should have been more, like, confrontational or whatever about it, because, as I know from hard time spent in the world of curating, more often than not, people like Trina are nothing more than cool-hunters, you know, dear Lee? They just wait it out until pals of theirs get behind something, something you may or may not call Avant-Garde, before jumping in all the way.

But none of that really happens—I've imagined it on the elevator ride down to the ground floor on the way to meet Trina.

How it really really goes is that I come out of the elevator and into the dining hall where a big, beautiful, buffet breakfast is being served. Trina, sitting at a table by herself near where the coffee urns are set up, and all I can really do is stand there in the doorway, watching.

I'm there for like five minutes, and I know I just can't do it, you know, Lee? I can't go through with the whole ordeal.

Maybe if it were some other time, or if I were someone other than myself.

There's sun coming in the windows, and there is that picture of Al Pittman behind the bar, with his pint of Guinness.

I can't move. I think of the fox we hit on the highway, how it couldn't raise its head from the muck in the gutter.

And then, Lee, sorry again, I just turn around and hit the UP button on the elevator, and boy, once inside, what a relief, this bitch is taken up like a ghost or an angel or something, right to the seventh floor and to my room.

—— • ——

So the sun has come up, now it goes back down.

The morning continental: grapefruit, sugar, croissant and coffee: last night I thought of hanging myself.

Supper: the Sea Shanty Bar & Grill: fresh salmon, chard, mash and lemon: a car wreck in the ditch by the highway.

I'm sad as a motherfucker, but so super pumped about the reading and this bizarre panel discussion (entitled WHY ARE WE SO TALENTED?) that even the Down Below is behaving itself—I dreamed dreams of cold running water all last night.

Catherine behind the podium.

"This is new writing," she says.

She's fidgety and keeps clearing her throat.

"The piece I'm about to read for you has to do with my own relationship to reading."

She pauses.

"I think all you need to know about it is that the person, 'Martin,' who I mention, is my husband."

Her eyes come up from the podium. I can see her searching for me in the crowd.

"On Reading," she says, shuffling her paper.

"I can't. I just CAN'T anymore. Reading is an abusive relationship. Who the fuck do these people think they are? These "writers." Writers?

Who's that? What kind of ludicrous ego do these people have? I hate them all. I'm ten lines into something and I think to myself: I'd rather have Martin eat my puss.

"I'm serious. I hate them. I hate the Romantics, the Modernists, the Postmodernists. I hate sensual women. I despise terse, spare, repressed men. I hate the ornate, I hate the baroque, I hate minimalism. I can't stand the Colonialists, and the Post-Colonialists make me wanna puke till my spine shatters.

"I hate prose. I hate poetry. I hate those fucking conceptual writers. What a bunch of chuckleheads they are. I hate satire. I hate tragedy. Everything is so boring and dumb. The idea of writing a script is akin to Auschwitz. Right through here, ladies and gents, and hit the switch, Fritz!

"I hate the whites. I hate the blacks. I hate the Jews. I hate the Russians, the Germans, the English, the Americans, the South and Central Americans, the sub Continental Asians, the Asians, I hate the literature of First Nations people. The Irish are some kind of venereal disease. And you know how I feel about those horrid Canadians.

"I hate the homosexuals. I hate the heterosexuals. I hate the trans-gendered and I even hate books for kids.

"I hate the Bible. I hate Shakespeare. If I have to sit through spoken word ever again, I'll kill.

"I hate non-fiction. I hate history. I fucking loathe whatever the hell 'Theory' is. Philosophy is like, whatever.

"I hate the literature of the oppressed. I hate the literature of the oppressors. I hate conservatives, and I fucking hate *the people.*

"I hate fairy tales. I hate grossly inverted feminist reworkings of fairy tales. I hate alienation, and I hate the socially conscious and engaged.

"And yet, I read. Abusive, right? Here I am, crawling back to you. I hate you I love you blah blah blah blah. After Martin's done flicking that little bean with his tongue, what happens?

"I look over at that bookshelf in my bedroom. Some stupid and just fucking beautiful line of poetry comes into my head. I reach out with my hand and my eyes and my dim-witted heart. I'm sorry, baby. The world's all right. Everything's shit, but it's all right, I say. It's just you and me, baby, I say. My hand, my eyes, my dim-witted heart.

"I turn out the light and go to sleep."

Applause. Catherine's face flushes. She smiles.

She takes a seat with the MC and the other reader on the stage.

I'm watching from the Cool Table. This is where Catherine was sitting before she read, and the other writer (Dude with bleached teeth, white high tops, a Tap Out tee, tear-drop tattoo, ball cap on the forty-fin (Yo—like, who really killed Tupac and Biggie?) whose name I can't recall, slouched here menacingly before he went on, and once on stage, to seem, I don't know, Lee, like techno-edge-y: read off his iPad—but now, the two of them up there on the stage with the MC at the Sea Shanty Bar & Grill (Surf and Turf $8.99!!!), their readings (during which my eyes bled: Dude rapped, Lee, he *rapped*: (*I'm rough/and tough/and I don't/give a fuck/'bout nudding . . ./cause I don't*)) having finished, I see that it's just me with Granny Powderbomb (Dear God, dear Lee, the makeup) Numbers One, Two and Three, with the host of the opening reception from last night occupying what appears to be the most prime real estate in the dingy confines of the dining hall.

WHY ARE WE SO TALENTED?

INTERVIEWER
So thanks to both of you so much for sharing your work with us tonight. There's really some great stuff on the go in there. As you know, this is the Dandelion's twenty-seventh year, and those of us who are real dinosaurs (har har) who're old enough to remember the very first festival are just so pleased with the way things have gone. One thing that really jumps out at you is just how much talent we have here

in Newfoundland and Labrador, and how, every year, whether it's in writing, or music, or painting, there are just so many new and compelling voices in the province.

So Catherine and Dude, you're both from here. You're both born and raised in Newfoundland and Labrador. Why do you think it is we produce so much outstanding talent compared to our relatively small population? Dude Whatever, why don't you go first?

DUDE WHATEVER
Sure, thanks for having me. I just want to say how thrilled I am to be a part of the Dandelion this year. I've been a fan for a long time, and it means a lot to me to have been invited finally.

I think a great deal of our identity, and the cultural production that follows from that, is connected to our sense of isolation. As an island, we in Newfoundland feel separate from the rest of Canada, from the rest of the world, really, and that leads us into some pretty interesting terrain artistically. We're a rugged and ragged lot. We're a proud people. We're rough-and-tumble. We've always sort of had to endure a lot of hardships, and I think that's a big part of who we are, and why we're as talented as we are.

INTERVIEWER
Catherine? Your thoughts? Do you agree with Dude that isolation plays such a role in our cultural life?

CATHERINE PRINCE
I don't really know about that. I think the basic assumption of the question is a matter for some debate, actually. I also think it's kinda remarkable and self-serving that here, at the Dandelion, a cultural event, we're being asked to publicly muse about what makes us all so great. I mean, the question should be: *Are* we that great?

INTERVIEWER

Well, just given our small population, and the quality of artists we produce.

DUDE WHATEVER

There's also the poverty. The poverty is a big deal. Ireland. That Irish tradition we have. I mean, we used to be our own fucking country! (*Laughter*)

That leads to us all having such bloody big chips on our shoulders. And the weather. The weather is terrible! (*Laughter*)

And then there's the seal hunt!

INTERVIEWER

But Catherine, I want to ask you: Don't you feel that Dude has a good point? That geography and history have played a role in how our culture has developed? That there's something unique happening here?

CATHERINE PRINCE

Well, whether something is unique is a different discussion than whether it's any good. But to answer your question, it's perfectly transparent: Yes. Yes, the context in which our culture has developed is because of our geography and history. That's like saying the sky is blue.

As for the quality of the artists we produce, I think posterity will ultimately be the judge. I'm unfortunately a bit of a Modernist in regards to this question. Criticality is vital. Frankly, there are very few artists from Newfoundland whose work I see as being of much interest beyond evidence of the dominance of bourgeois culture.

INTERVIEWER

Why do you hate Newfoundland so much?

CATHERINE PRINCE
What? I don't hate Newfoundland.

DUDE WHATEVER
My work is far from middle-class. My work is of the streets. My work is gritty and real. It's like really real.

CATHERINE PRINCE
I haven't read your work. But from your performance tonight, I'd have to say that you, sir, are just trying way too hard.

INTERVIEWER
Just answer my question. Why do you hate your home?

That's how it goes, more or less. It's like the best panel discussion I've ever seen. But something about the whole thing has made me even more sad than I was before.

I'm watching Catherine. I'm watching her say the things I've always wanted her to say. I'm so proud of her. Up there on the stage, she's just the person I've always wanted her to be, but she's also the person she always has been: the Real Troublemaker, that tough little bitch, that critical witch, the pure magic, the real gold and the blood and the real dangerous stuff—not the fake, the phony, the fraud—it's her, Catherine, up there on the stage.

She looks down at me, out through that circle of light she's in, that halo, that golden noose, and she's smiling at me, and I don't want to, but I'm thinking about the statue of Shawnadithit.

I'm up and out, knocking into Granny Powderbomb Number Three as I go, outside the Sea Shanty and into the warm night, where there, in the parking lot, just as the door closes behind me, I see a cab pull up, and in the dome light glow spilling out from the inside of the car, Martin is taking his bags from the trunk.

I don't know if he sees me, Lee, but anyway, I don't stop to say Hi or whatever, I just kinda keep to the shadows, pull my collar up blah blah, and find myself walking away from the hotel and the pub to where I'm not even sure.

Through some huge, dim graveyard, the roots from the overhanging trees pushing up through the path in front of me: church steeple, moon, low clouds just gunning it right across the open sky, the light a perfect indigo, and indigo my hands in the dark, later, as somehow, I've found my way through the little town to the main door of the art school, its windows likewise dark except there through the glass where I see the bloody red spill from the EXIT sign above a doorway down some empty hall.

And, by chance, round the back of the school (I remember that beautiful smoking area of Heart), a door propped open with a cinder block, an accident of the faulty memory of some elderly maintenance man—a near-retiree preoccupied with the memories of his long-lost daughter who drowned forty years ago—who broke through ice while skating, the blades like two silver hooks flashing in the moonlight as the ice shattered beneath her, and all these long years later, thinking of her—the deepest indigo of the water which took her down quick as anything—there wasn't even a cry from her and she was gone, and thereafter the ruin of his marriage, his drinking, his bachelor apartment across from the college wherein at night he sits watching the hockey game and hearing the sound of skate blades cutting ice—all this taking up his concentration so that he forgot all about propping that door open, and is now, maybe, for all I know, dear Lee, back at the Sea Shanty Bar & Grill listening to Catherine.

And I'm standing in some darkened room with my hands out in front of me, feeling my way around and smelling the turpentine, the oils, graphite, paper, rubber, charcoal. Photo chemicals thick in the air like a bomb just went off, everything burned black.

A wide open studio, where it looks like Figure Drawing 101 takes place. Bodies rendered either well or not at all well, variously posed, falling through space or otherwise frozen. A hand, an eye, a dim-witted heart.

A car passes outside, and I don't hear the tires screech, I don't hear the hideous crunch of crumpled metal, shattered glass and bone. There's nothing but the sound of my own heart, still beating, my breath, the blood running yet through the veins and arteries—no fierce wind blowing, just so, against the windows, nor, for that matter, whistling through the tops of the trees outside blah blah—there's nothing, that is to say, but me, dear Lee, standing here, still alive and waiting in the dark.

DAY. SIX.

Portland Creek

The next day I see her and Martin in the parking lot outside the hotel loading up their luggage for the long, prolonged, scenic, post-pop-the-question drive all the way back to St. John's, to and fro.

And there is no doubt: it's popped. I can see it in her face.

Look, dear Lee, I'm an educated guy, as I've mentioned. I know all about the banality of evil, you know? I believe in the labour movement. I light a candle on the night of the anniversary of the Haymarket Massacre (actually, I don't). But when I see Martin's face in the bright spring sunlight outside the hotel, his khaki pants and his Lacoste shirt, his whole business-casual thing, a beaming Catherine beside him, I give up hope for anything resembling something even somewhat having to do with a meaningful existence.

Their shadows a couple of black construction paper cut-outs on the pavement as they come toward me, both smiling. I stand outside the lobby with my bags saying, Hello Martin, nice to see you, while a shockwave of pain up that white ladder, my spine, does climb and recede from whence it came. That is, dear Lee, well you know.

Some words are exchanged. Martin's flight was pleasant, he asks if I'd like some drugs, some psychedelics for my upcoming time in the wilderness.

I grip the Thunderbolt.

"Not really my thing," I say.

"What happened to you last night?" Catherine says. "I looked all over for you."

"Went for a walk."

I scan the parking lot and the street beside the hotel, my heart set to burst in a shower of white light, like a time-lapse lily blooming, some supernova behind the dark clutch of my rib cage.

We load the luggage into the car.

Quickly, I think, quickly.

I'm like, Get me the fuck out of here.

Catherine waves So Long to the smokestack and its chemical plume as we pull out of town. Heading north, not, dear Lee, to that distant stretch of spruce where your plane went down, but only a few hours drive from here, to Portland Creek, where it all started for you: in just another ramshackle town where the salmon run and you first learned the meaning of gravity in your tiny twin-engine, how the molten burning heart of the world never ceases to call and grasp with invisible fingers your bones and the very marrow of your bones and to pull you down from the crisp air into the underground where there's nothing, dear Lee, thank God, thereafter, but the darkness and heat of a world that's forgotten you.

It's different now. Martin behind the wheel, and instead of the swerves, the crazy fast accelerations, the sudden, spine-shattering–WE'RE ALL GOING TO DIE–screeching, shuddering stops, it's a cautious plod.

The mountainous terrain around us. The air so dry you feel your nose might start to gush blood or whatever. Higher elevation—up up we go. The wild blue yonder. Huge clouds are white and grey. And always, that road, now winding, now straight, pulls us along.

Martin, like Catherine, is just rocking out to that folk music, I mean he's just totally into it: the two of them up front, stealing glances at one another, singing along to the CD, harmonizing on the choruses, and in the window, there's the reflection of my face, dear Lee, and it doesn't look good.

It doesn't look good—for any of us. Doc Sparling once said to me: You seem to have an inordinate amount of dread in your life.

Don't we all, don't we all.

I remember at the funeral, breaking things down for Catherine in a manner that suggested I'd finally lost it for good:

At 7:04, we argued.

7:18, she called the clinic.

7:33, she started to pack up her things.

8:01, I watched the car pull away.

8:03, weeping.

8:10, whisky and weeping.

8:15, same.

Thereafter, same.

Catherine said, later, at that morbid First Anniversary party for two we'd had: That's how we deal with those kinda things: we get all factual. We say, This is how it happened, you know? We lay out the time things happen, moment by moment, to try to make sense of it.

In front of us on the road, an enormous RV with a bumper sticker saying: RETIRED ENGLISH PROF, and another one: I CAN'T GO ON I'LL GO ON.

Driving along, I had planned on us finding something truly symbolic here, you know, Lee? Like, me, Catherine and Martin maybe coming to some little farm on the way north—a pen of stunted Newfoundland ponies or whatever with a farmer version of Harry Sullivan letting us feed carrots to them through the gaps of the fence and the pleasure of their wet lips on our hands et cetera. And then, maybe, late at night, here's me unable to sleep, leaving the motel room we'd rented nearby and walking roadside back to the farm—a big, bloody moon above my head—I'd think about Jess and the night she died or whatever—something melancholy yet shot through with hope of some kind—and finally coming to the pen where the ponies sleep standing upright in the dark, I'd unlatch the gate and open it wide for them only to realize that they would never leave—that they're content and happy in the prison that was made for them.

But it doesn't happen that way, of course. Life doesn't have the courtesy for something even as small as that—it's just the three of us onward over the road in the Crown Royal.

And it'll be years from now, when I'll look back at this sweet, quick drive in the late afternoon sun to Portland Creek with Martin and Catherine, the towering trees and the mountains around us, them newly engaged, you, dear Lee, whispering to me all across this wasteland—years and years from now—again, in that other book—another country, another holocaust—I'll get nostalgic for the sadness I'm feeling right now, listening to those two do their harmonies up front, thinking of Jess and the horrible and simple heartbreak of things—this trip will seem like relief.

And now, maybe here's the saddest part of this whole mess—the trip, the Dandelion, Catherine and Martin in a call-and-respond up front ("Lord let me die with a hammer in my hand")—we're here, I mean, we're here, and it's not like I hadn't seen the photos online when I made my reservation: one un-serviced campsite beside the river with the big hills of Portland Creek crowding down—but God damn, Lee—I see just how inhabited your former home is—the roads and the houses, the campsites, the cabins, over that hill trees cut for the nearby mill, the welcome centre where I hand over my credit card, the distant buzz of traffic even here in the greenery—that is, commerce, money, there's no escape, Lee—everything's bought and sold, to and fro, life it tends to come and go—Catherine's mouth I see in the side-view mirror singing not the words she's literally singing, Lee, but rather some other language, some code words I just don't get—it's over and done with, move on, she's saying, except not, except yes, that is what she's saying—and we've arrived at the end.

—— • ——

Feel less alone in the world.
Observe how others do it, and follow suit.
Feel connected to nature.
Feel connected to your fellow humans.
Observe, and follow suit.

Martin kills the engine of the car. I see through the window the trees stretching back over the hills into the distance. A path leads through the underbrush down to the edge of the water, and I take my things from the trunk, Catherine and Martin waiting as I shoulder my pack and pick up my fly rod from where I leaned it against the fender.

The two of them exchange a few quiet words I can't catch, and Martin comes over to me, his face a red blotch like a stain of wine on a table cloth.

"Well, see you later," he says. "We'll have to have you over sometime when you get back to town." He puts out his chubby little paw. "We're going down to Mexico for a few days, but we should have you over." He kind of smiles and grimaces. I see Catherine's face over his shoulder.

A warm overcast windy day. Her eyes the colour of the mud in the path that leads down to the water. To what I'm not even sure, dear Lee, though this whole trip I've been thinking about it. I know what I'd planned for when I arrived here, but now there's something else.

"Come on," she says, "at least let me walk you the first few steps."

She loops her arm through the crook of my elbow. Takes my rod to carry. It's a long way down to the bottom. There's a hill we go down and jutting up from the muddy path are white teeth of rock.

Light rain falling. The sound of our feet squelching in the mud. I watch her face in profile as we walk, the greenery behind her. In the trees, the yellow jewel of a finch.

End of the path. A river through branches. She lays her head gently on my shoulder as we watch the water break and jetty.

"Wish I could go with you," she says.

"Don't lie," I say. "But I wish you could too."

We stand there for a while like that not saying anything.

She kisses my cheek.

Then I go down the path silently to where the river waits.

—— • ——

I dig a small pit in the ground with my hand, and fill it with dead grass, peels of bark from a birch tree, little sticks.

> Next, a teepee of broken limbs from nearby trees.
> I strike a match, and push the little flame into the tinder.
> A ghost of smoke rises up.
> Once it's caught: dead red boughs, splits of wood.
> The big logs at last.
> The water in them sizzles from the heat.
> I look at the fire for a long time, the river.
> In the far-off distance, an engine starts and is silent.
> I take the book from my backpack.
> It burns instantly—I watch sparks and flakes of ash drift up into the sky.
> I'll go with nothing—a heart, my hands.

That night, I look out at where the river runs into the pond, and there on the surface where the moon shines down all silver. Out there I see you coming up from the ground on the far side and you're walking on the water.

All of you—Jess, the baby with angel wings, and Catherine and Martin, holding hands. There's this kind of sound like singing. And behind you all there's Harry Sullivan, Trina, GoD and Dick Evans and Johnny Xerox too. My dad even. Maybe everyone I've ever known. Maybe everyone. You all seem to come up from under the ground on the far side of the pond. The whole lot of you walking toward me on the surface of the water, and there's this glow to you all. I can see it.

I can see this beautiful glow. The voices are raised up, echoing through the wild trees. And I see how all of your hands are locked together. I can just barely make you out, but I see those hands, and the glow, and that sound like singing coming to me.

And I'm looking out at the reflection of the waning moon on the water, and then I watch the moon itself—across the sky, coming down to the horizon—I'm watching it, now obscured by the mist that sits upon the tops of the distant trees—the treetops now in silhouette against it—the moon descending, creeping down—it's barely visible now—I'm watching it disappear—slowly and silently—it's nearly gone—a silver edge above the trees—disappearing—it's gone.

NOTES.

Quote on page 34 from "What Animals Are," in "The Analytical Language of John Wilkins," Jorge Luis Borges

Joanna Rees, 2015

Craig Francis Power is an artist and writer from St. John's, Newfoundland, Canada. His first novel, *Blood Relatives* (Pedlar Press 2010), won the Percy Janes First Novel Award, the Fresh Fish Award for Emerging Writers, the ReLit Award, and was short-listed for the BMO Winterset Award. His hooked rugs, installations, and videos have shown widely across Canada and internationally in both solo and group exhibitions. In 2008, Power was nominated for the Sobey Art Award, which recognizes the work of Canadian artists under forty.